I0547818

TOCABAGA 9

THE CRIMSON CROSS

THOMAS H. WARD

TOCABAGA 9:

THE CRIMSON CROSS

by

THOMAS H. WARD

ISBN-13: 978-0692402337

ISBN-10: 0692402330

Copyright © 2015. All rights reserved. No part of this publication may be reproduced, distributed, or transmitted in any form or by any means, including photocopying, recording, or other electronic mechanical methods.

This book is a work of fiction. Names, characters, and incidents are a product of the author's imagination or used fictitiously. Any resemblance to persons, living or dead is entirely coincidental.

Transcendent Publishing
www.transcendentpublishing.com

PREFACE

If you've been reading my chronicles then you know all the problems that we run into almost everyday. The Tocabaga security forces are on full alert due to the Ebola threat. We can't afford to let new people on the island because they may be contagious.

Hordes of people are moving to Florida from the northern states. They bring crime, trouble, and death with them. We've heard they're fleeing the northern states due to the climate change. The weather has become unseasonably cold. The Hordes create many problems, but the main one is over-population causing food shortages.

We have to be alert and ready to fight to keep our way of life safe. Someday the country will return to the rule of law and liberty under the United States Constitution. Until that day returns we must endeavor to persevere.

My name is Jack Gunn, and these are my chronicles.

RECAP OF JULY 14, 2025, MY LAST ENTRY

SOMETIME AFTER MIDNIGHT

It was a busy night. We raided the Green Zone clinic, fighting our way in and out, and captured the much needed anti-Ebola vaccine EVB150. Some of Rico's men had Ebola so we decided to take him the necessary doses. When we arrived at the 54th Avenue Bridge we found that Rico's compound was completely engulfed in flames.

The fire was so hot we stopped 200 feet away. I told my crew to stay with the trucks while I checked it out. I phoned Rico but there was no answer.

I managed to move within 100 feet of the front door at the main building but the heat was too intense. I saw shadows running away from the fire in the other direction. Then two men and a woman came running over to me. Their clothes were burned in places and maybe their bodies. I couldn't tell because of the black soot on their faces and hands. They were within 15 feet of me when I pointed my gun in their direction.

I warned them, "Don't come any closer."

They stopped in their tracks. "Have any of you seen Rico?"

One of them said, "Hey, aren't you Jack Gunn?"

"Yeah. What the hell is going on here?"

The woman replied, "They're killing everyone. Please let us go, we don't mean you any harm."

I lowered my M4 and they took off running. I shouted, "Who's killing everyone?" They kept running and didn't look back.

Moving closer to the fire I yelled, "Rico … Rico!"

I stood there holding my hand up to cover my face from the heat. I yelled again for my friend. People running around inside the compound trying to escape. They were trying to climb the razor wire fence.

I stood there as long as I could and then backed away from the heat. I heard several explosions and the crack of bullets going off from the heat. I noticed dead bodies lying on the street. They appeared to have been shot, but I couldn't tell. I sure as hell wasn't going to touch them because they might be infected.

Suddenly the 10 foot high fence collapsed from the heat and five men rushed out at me. When they approached I shouted, "Stop! Don't come any closer or I'll shoot."

They didn't respond, so I started to slowly back away from them. They looked like zombies. They were in shock for sure. I yelled again but they kept coming. Moving backwards, I tripped over something in the street and fell on my ass.

When I fell, they rushed towards me. I scrambled, managing to swing my M4 in their direction, and opened fire on full automatic. I sprayed rounds back and forth, as they dropped to the ground five feet away. I kept scooting backwards, on my butt, to make sure I was out of their reach.

That was too close for comfort. Thank God, none of them touched me. I breathed a sigh of relieve, stood up, and brushed off my pants. I wondered if they were trying to kill me, take my gun, or what.

I yelled some more for Rico. After half an hour of yelling and peering into the flames I walked back to the vehicles. "Let's get the hell out of here! I couldn't find Rico. Maybe he's dead."

No one said a word as we drove back to

Tocabaga except for Tommy. He asked me, "What do you think happened?"

"I don't know. I just don't know what happen."

We arrived back on Tocabaga and put the vaccine in a refrigerated storage unit. The eight of us went to the Green Room for a much needed drink. Tony poured us all a double shot. We held up the glasses for a toast and looked at each other, not saying a word. After downing the booze, I said, "Good job guys. I'm beat. See y'all later."

I went home, took a shower, and went to bed. It was just turning daylight as I crawled into bed trying not to wake my wife. She softly asked me, "You ok?"

"Yeah, I'm ok. I just need some sleep." She lightly rubbed my shoulder. The one that always hurts from the fight I had with al-Qaida terrorists. Ever since I fell into a 10-foot pit it has never been the same. It hurts like hell when I raise my left arm.

I'm glad she didn't ask me more questions because I didn't feel like talking. I didn't want to think about what happen to Rico or I'd never fall asleep.

I closed my eyes and tried not to think about

the new Invisible enemy.

JULY 14, 2025 CONTINUED

I woke up late in the day. It was almost 5 pm as I went downstairs for some much needed grub. Hemmi said, "Tommy told me that Rico was missing."

I gave her a kiss and replied, "Yeah, his whole compound was burned to the ground. I phoned him but he didn't answer. I searched the whole area for him."

"Well, you did your best. He's probably around somewhere. Like you always say, he's the toughest man you know."

"Yeah, maybe you're right."

Hemmi stood there with her apron on. "What would you like to eat?"

"It doesn't matter."

She whipped up some fried fish and flat bread along with a few oranges.

While eating I told her, "I gotta call Sessions today and advise him that we got the Ebola vaccine. Tomorrow, I wanna go search for Rico again."

"You just need to take it easy," she said.

"Where is everyone?"

"The kids are out playing and I think the guys are on guard duty."

I grabbed a cup of coffee laced with JD and went out on the patio for a smoke. I pushed the speed dial on my cell to call Sessions. "Captain, I have some good news. We captured 30,000 doses of EVB150. They're in refrigerated storage, until you pick them up."

"That's great news, Jack. We're in Miami getting ready to assault the Federal Bank tonight. There's a lot of Feds here, but I think they'll surrender without a fight. When we have the vaccine we'll fly it to SOCOM for distribution. I'll send a chopper to Tocabaga to pick up the doses you have in a few days."

"Captain, if it's ok, I'd like to keep 1,000 units here just in case. We went to Rico's compound yesterday to give some out. The whole place was on fire. A lot of people were killed. Rico is missing."

"What happened to him?"

"I don't know."

"Sorry to hear that. I know you were good friends."

"Yeah, I hate to think about it."

Sessions said, "After we secure the vaccine we're moving out to the Keys. The objective is to mop up any Chinese Military still lurking around. Oh, by the way, we sank that invisible gunboat yesterday."

"That's good to hear. Good luck, Captain." That was the end of our conversation.

I pushed Rico's speed dial but there was no answer.

I thought something terrible has happened to Rico and his family. Maybe they became infected. Maybe they died in the fire or someone killed them. I have to find out what happened.

I jumped in my truck and did a quick tour of the island checking on my security forces. Everything seemed in order and most of the men were in good spirits.

Arriving at the Green Room I found all my men from the night before, along with Doc Scott. Doc said, "Tomorrow at 10 am is the service for Albert. You need to say a few words."

I said, "Yeah, of course I will. By the way, how's his wife and kids doing? Will they be there?"

"They're great so far. There's no sign of any fever. I'm setting up a live video feed for them to watch at home. I don't think it's a good idea they attend. A lot of people are worried about becoming infected."

"Yeah, we have to keep them in quarantine."

I said, "Tommy, pour your old Dad a drink." He knows what I like and handed me a double shot of JD with a water chaser.

I lit up a smoke and took a sip of JD. It burned going down, but it tasted so good. I like to sip my booze to enjoy the favor. I looked at the group and said, "I need two volunteers to go with me to search for Rico after the service tomorrow."

No one said a word except for Army Mike. "Count me in, Jack."

Tommy replied, "I don't think that's a good idea, but I'll go along."

"We won't take any chances. It'll be a quick trip," I said.

"You're right it's going to be a quick trip. I don't wanna be hanging around an infected zone,"

Mike commented.

Doc asked me, "What are you going to do if you find Rico? What if he already has Ebola?"

I took another sip of whiskey and a drag on my smoke. These were good questions.

"Yeah, what are we going to do?" Mike asked.

I looked around at everyone and said, "Here's my thinking. If we find Rico or anyone we can't come in contact with them. Most likely everyone has been exposed to Ebola. We can't help them. All we can do is provide some food and water."

Doc butted in, "You could check them for a fever. If they don't have a fever then they're not contagious. Then you could give them the oral vaccine EVB150. I have two infrared thermometers you can use so you don't have to touch anyone. If they have a fever over 101, then it's too late for the vaccine."

"Ok, good thinking, Doc. We'll need some rubber gloves just in case," I advised.

Tommy commented, "Let's take some Hazmat suits along."

I said, "No. Hazmat suits just make you feel over-confident. Then you take stupid risks. We'll take 100 doses of vaccine, rubber gloves, and the thermometers. We're going there to find Rico and his family, not to save everyone. Anyone who has a fever or shows signs of Ebola, we put them out of their misery. That includes Rico."

Doc advised, "Remember, Ebola can live up to 60 days in a dead body. I recommend that you burn any bodies using gasoline."

"That's a good point. We'll bring along five gallons of gas. Anything else?" No one responded.

"Ok, if nothing else let's get some food."

Tommy and I went home for dinner and went to bed early. Tomorrow would be another crazy day. There's no telling how long we would be gone or what would happen.

JULY 15, 2025

We had a memorial service for Albert. I was disappointed that only a few people showed up to show their respects. Not many people actually knew Albert since he was more or less new here. They didn't know he served in the Navy.

They didn't know he was a kind man. All he wanted to do was help others who were sick or injured. That's why he became a medic. In my eyes Albert was a hero who gave his life to protect the people of this community. I'll make sure he gets a white cross in our little Tocabaga grave yard. Everyone who dies here gets a white cross unless they were a bad guy.

After the service Mike, Tommy, and I drove to Rico's compound. We arrived only to find smoldering ashes and a lot of dead bodies in the street. In the daylight we could see that most of the dead had been shot. The stench was horrible so we covered our faces with surgical masks to reduce the smell and provide some protection in case the disease was airborne.

We drove around the perimeter of the destroyed compound and counted 54 bodies. We poured gas on them and lit them up. There were more dead people inside the compound but we didn't dare go inside. The area was still hot with small fires burning inside.

The main building was a pile of bricks with one wall still standing. Judging by the damage and the intensity of the fire this place was fire-bombed. Some kind of fuel had to be used to burn down a brick building.

It was like a burned out ghost town. It gave me the creeps. There was nothing else we could do so we decided to mount up and leave. We wanted to get out of the danger zone.

As we drove back over the 54th Avenue Bridge, which crosses Interstate 275, Tommy stopped the truck and pointed. "Look."

Down the road we could see a group of people heading south, towards us, about one mile away. It was a large group, which I estimated to be around a 1,000 people. Most were on foot, but there were a few vehicles. I pulled out my binoculars and gazed at the horde.

Slowly scanning the rag-tag group I saw it was made up of men, women, and children. They were moving in a formation. They had scouts in the front and a rear guard. The majority of the women and children were in the center of the formation.

Men located on the perimeter all carried some type of weapon. I couldn't make out the exact types, but some had rifles.

Tommy said, "Let me have a look."

I commented, "They seem well organized."

As Tommy viewed the horde he commented, "Yeah, but it looks like a scout spotted us."

I grabbed the spy glasses for a look-see. A scout on a motorcycle was pointing at us from about a half mile away. He spotted us alright.

I handed Mike the glasses for a look. "The cycle is coming our way."

"Let's leave before we have a run in with them," I said. Tommy mashed the gas and we took off.

Mike commented, "I wonder where they're from."

"I wonder where they're going." I replied.

"I hope they aren't coming to Tocabaga," Tommy replied. "That's a large group. They probably have 400 fighters."

"I think you're right. I hope the poor fools

don't stop at Rico's compound."

No one else said a word as we drove home. We all knew that if the horde stopped at the compound it could mean death for the entire group.

Arriving at Tocabaga I had Tommy and Mike go to the Fort and set up the radar system. We needed this to detect any boats coming to the area. The radar would be set-up in the HQ radio room. It would be monitored 24-7 by two men. If the radar detected any boats then a radio call would be sent out to our rapid reaction force.

Our rapid response team is made up of 20 men who are on call all the time. It has four teams with five men in each one. Each team has one light machine gun and everyone carries an M4. The two Hummers with the 50 caliber guns are at their disposal. Of course Tommy, Rick, Mike, and I are members of the rapid reaction force.

While the radar was being installed I looked for Rick. I found him at the Green Room. It was almost 5 pm. I asked Tony for a drink. Sitting on the floor next to Rick was one of his German Shepherds.

Rick has two big German Shepherd guard dogs. He keeps them at home most of the time for his wife and kid's protection. These dogs are smart, protective, and oddly enough friendly to most people. Dogs like this can sense who's a friend and who isn't. They are unique well-trained dogs.

Rick asked, "Did you find Rico?"

"There were just dead bodies and no Rico."

"That's too bad."

"Oh, I almost forgot. We saw a horde of people moving south on 275."

"What do mean a horde?"

"It looked like about a thousand people. There were men, women, and kids moving south in a rag-tag military formation."

"Shit, I hope they don't find our location," Rick said.

"Yeah, I agree." Looking at Rick's dog I said, "It's too bad we don't have more dogs like Klaus here."

Upon hearing his name Klaus walked over to me with his tail wagging. I rubbed his head and he sat down next to me.

Rick looked at me and commented, "I could breed my dogs if I had some new blood."

"Maybe we could find a dog running around out there," I said.

"Why do you wanna do that?" Rick asked.

"I wanna use them for security. Remember when the al-Qaida terrorists infiltrated here? We could have used dogs to find them. Hell, we could have used dogs to find the Invisibles."

"If we can find the right dog we could breed them. It has to be a male or female Shepherd that's no older than four or five years," Rick said.

"Where could we find a dog like that?"

"Years ago, there was a Shepherd breeder not far from here. Over in Gulfport. I purchased my dog Heidi from him. She's the best dog I have."

"Maybe he's still there and we can buy one from him," I replied.

Tony poured us both another drink. Rick commented, "Let's go tomorrow and check it out."

"Ok, sounds good."

Tony said, "If you don't mind, I'll come along."

I replied, "Good, we'll all go. Let's leave at 9 am."

We all had one more drink and headed home. Before going home I stopped by the main bridge to check things out. Chris was the head man on duty. I walked up and asked, "Everything ok?"

"Yep, everything is fine."

I pulled out two smokes and offered him one. Then wind was blowing from the north and it sent a little chill down my spine. A full moon was shining as I looked down the main road.

I thought I saw something move across the street about half a mile away. I stared down the road, squinting, trying to see what it was. I looked for a minute or two not saying a word.

Chris asked, "You see something?"

"It was probably just a coyote."

We finished the smoke and I bid Chris a good night, but warned him. "Keep your eyes open. You know there's a horde of people out there somewhere."

He nodded his head. "Yeah, I heard."

My sixth sense told me something was out there lurking in the dark.

JULY 16, 2025

We bugged out of Tocabaga exactly at 9 am. I had already informed my family and the bridge security where we were going.

As we drove down the road, leaving the island, I told Rick to go slow. Approaching the spot where I thought I saw something last night we stopped. I got out and looked around the area. I didn't see anything in the street so I walked down to the mangrove trees at the edge of the water.

Rick asked, "What the hell are you looking for?"

I advised, "I don't know. I thought I saw someone here last night."

As I looked in the soft sand I found what I was looking for. Fresh foot-prints were all over the place. The prints indicated that about four people where here. Someone was checking us out.

I advised Rick and Tony about the foot-prints. They could belong to Free Roamers or anybody. Just the same, we agreed to put our security on alert. We continued on our way after a brief discussion.

We were headed to Gulfport which was a 15 mile drive; located in Pinellas County right next to St. Petersburg. It used to be a small middle-class city made up of all kinds of people. Gulfport was primarily noted for being an artist community.

The last time we went to Gulfport was when we followed the Boko Kang Gang looking for Brogan, who was MIA. At the time, we drove through it and didn't stop to look around.

Rick stopped the truck in the middle of the downtown area. We observed a few people walking around the boarded up stores. When they saw our truck flying the Stars and Stripes they shied away from us. None of them appeared to be a physical threat. On the other hand they could have Ebola so we didn't take any chances and kept an eye on them.

I asked, "Why are we stopping?"

Rick replied, "I'm trying to get my bearings. If I remember correctly the breeder's name was Tummel. I think he lived on 58th Street, on the corner of 11th Avenue."

Ten minutes later we pulled up to a house that had large kennels in the fenced-in backyard.

I said, "Tony, stay with the truck while we

go look around."

Rick and I jumped out with our M4's and walked up to the front door. It was wide open so we walked in. Rick yelled, "Mr. Tummel!" There was no reply. He yelled again. "Anyone here?" Again there was no reply.

I didn't like the situation so I flipped my safety off. We cleared each room in the little single story house. We found bags and bags of dog food scattered about the entire place. Dog crap was everywhere. The house stunk from the fifthly mess.

Looking out the back door we spotted the kennels and walked towards them. The entire yard was over-grown with thick, high weeds and bushes.

I noticed there were trails of trampled down grass that led to the kennels and the back porch. It indicated that someone or something had been regularly moving through this area. As we walked around the kennels we observed the cage doors were all open. No dogs were inside.

Rounding the corner of the last kennel we found human skeletal remains in the high grass. I saw a wallet on the ground and picked it up. Flipping it open I read the driver's license. It was Mr. Tummel's. We couldn't prove the body was his because it was so badly decomposed, but we assumed it was.

Rick said, "I wonder what happened here?"

"It looks like someone killed him. Maybe his dogs got him," I said.

"No, his dogs wouldn't attack him."

"Check his shirt for bullet holes," I replied.

Rick bent down and looked at his shirt. "There's not much of it left, but these look like bullet holes."

I glanced over at the shirt. "Yeah, it looks like someone killed him and took his dogs."

"It seems that way, but I doubt anyone could take the dogs."

"Oh, why's that?"

"Tummel trained these dogs. They were bred and trained to be guard dogs. They would never go with a stranger. If anything they would chase the person away or kill them."

I gave a doubtful look to Rick. "How do you know that?"

"Tummel trained my dogs and taught me how to train dogs. Tummel's dogs only understand

German. Unless you know the key German command words you're shit out of luck trying to control his dogs. I spent a considerable amount of time here learning how to train them."

Standing there, gazing around, I pointed to the pushed down grass trails. "What do you make of these trails?"

"It looks like someone comes here a lot," Rick replied. "Let's follow one." Rick picked a trail and I followed behind him. We were about 50 feet from the kennels when he stopped walking. "Here's another body," Rick said.

Rick stepped aside and I saw what was left of the body. "It looks like he was ripped apart," I said.

Rick commented, "I guarantee if he's the man who shot Tummel then the dogs got him."

I was looking around the area and saw a severed boney hand in the weeds holding a pistol. I picked up the gun and showed it to Rick. "This has to be the guy who killed Tummel."

"Now we know what happen to Tummel, but where are the dogs?" Rick asked.

We turned around and walked past the kennels to the back door. I was going up the squeaky steps when I heard low growls. Peeking inside I saw two wolf dogs, in a low crouch, coming towards me growling and snarling. They had incredibility large canine teeth. Their black eyes looked evil and seemed to stare right through you.

Rick heard the growls and softly said, "Don't run. Don't point your gun at them. Don't look directly into their eyes."

"They know what a gun is?" I asked.

"Of course they do. They're trained to know."

Then I heard growls behind us. I slowly, very slowly, turned my head to see two more Shepherds baring their teeth, standing in the yard. They were just a few feet away from Rick.

German Shepherds were formerly known as the Alsatian Wolf Dog in Europe.

Rick commented, "Don't move a muscle, Jack. I got this ... I think."

"You think? You better know for sure. I don't wanna get ate by a herd of German

Shepherds."

I moved my finger to the trigger while holding my M4 in a low ready position. If these dogs charged us I knew we would get bit before we could shoot them all.

Rick spoke in a deep commanding voice. "Nein!" The dogs stopped growling. They titled their heads while looking at Rick. That got their attention.

"Sitz!" To my amazement they all sat. A few of them started to whine a little. "Platz!" As if by magic the dogs all laid down while closely watching us.

One of the dogs, a huge mutt, started to get up. Rick pointed at it and yelled, "Platz, bleib!" The dog laid right back down.

Rick said, "Each dog still has a collar so maybe we can find out their names."

"You're doing a good job, so go ahead and check them. I'll watch you from here."

As Rick slowly moved closer to one dog he said, "Remember to speak in German. They don't understand English."

Step by step he approached the big Shepherd

repeating the following words, "Braver hund. Bleib. Repeating these words, the dog laid there and let Rick approach him. Rick held out his hand, palm down, for the dog to smell him. Then, not making any sudden moves, he petted the dog several times and looked at the collar.

The Shepherds looked like fearsome wild wolves. They were dirty and had matted hair. You could tell they'd been running wild for some time.

"You're not going to believe this. His name is Adolf," Rick advised. "Braver Hund, Adolf." Suddenly Adolf sat up, wagged his tail, and licked Rick's face. "He remembers me."

"Why would you name a dog Adolf?" I asked.

"He named it Adolf as a joke. Mr. Tummel use to say, 'I can boss Adolf Hitler around.' Tummel was German and he hated Hitler. Anyway this is the Alpha male. He rules this pack. If we control him then we control the pack."

"Which one is the Alpha female?"

"I'm guessing this one." He pointed to the dog next to Adolf and started moving slowly towards it, repeating the words: braver hund, bleib.

Once again he held out his hand for the dog

to smell. He stroked the matted fur and looked at the collar. "This one is Britta." As he said her name, she licked his hand.

"Rick, what the hell are we going to do with all these dogs?"

"You wanted guard dogs. Now we have a whole pack."

"Most people don't know how to speak any German."

"I'll teach everyone the command words. There's only a few of them. After a month of training the dogs will also understand English."

I looked at all the dogs and said, "We can't let these dogs run around Tocabaga. There's no telling what they'd do."

I know how dangerous big dogs can be if not correctly trained. I was a dog handler in the Military Police. Usually a dog becomes dangerous because the owner doesn't know how to train or handle them. I've owned big and small dogs. I love dogs because they're man's best friend, but they are still animals that can turn if provoked. Dogs study your body movements. They can tell by your movements and by smell if you are a friend or not.

I remember when my daughter was four years old and the neighbor's German Shepherd got loose. I heard her scream 'Daddy' so I ran outside. The dog had my daughter on the ground growling and was getting ready to bite her. I jumped off the porch and grabbed the dog by the throat getting it in a strangle-hold.

While holding the dog I told her to get in the house. The 70-pound dog was fighting for its life. I squeezed with all my strength while holding it on the ground until it stopped squirming around. The dog finally submitted to me. I had several bites and my arms were bleeding. I took the Shepherd back to its owner. This wasn't the first time this dog attacked my kids. I warned the owner the next time I'd kick his ass and shoot the dog.

Another run-in I had was when a Pit Bull attacked my wife's Toy Poodle. I grabbed the dog but it wouldn't let go of the poodle. I had to kick it in the head. Finally it let go and ran away. Our little poodle had to have 70 stitches from the mauling.

Rick said, "Look, the dogs aren't going to run around Tocabaga. We'll get volunteers from the security team to train and take care of them. We'll hold training sessions until the dogs are familiar with their new owners."

I said, "Hey, these two dogs just got up."

Rick pointed his finger at them and said, "Komm!" The Shepherds hesitated while looking at me and then at Rick. Rick lowered his voice and sternly repeated the word. I moved back, a couple of steps, out of their way. The dogs slinked by me and went to Rick. He ordered them to sit, stay.

Rick told me, "Look around for some leashes while I put them in the kennels."

I went in the house and started to search around. I was looking in the kitchen when I heard Rick yell, "No, down!" He repeated it several times and then he yelled, "Jack, help!"

I ran to the door and saw the two wolf dogs had Rick on the ground. One was standing right over his chest. Rick was holding the Shepherd back with both hands. The other one had buried his teeth into Rick's lower leg. It was definitely doing some damage. Rick was kicking the dog to stop the attack.

The commotion made the other dogs active. They were standing up watching the action. Rick was yelling commands in English trying to get the two crazy dogs to obey. They didn't listen to him.

Rick shouted to me, "They won't stop!"

I said, "Remember, speak in German."

Rick yelled commands in German and the dogs stopped the attack.

I ran over, grabbed each dog by its collar, and pulled them away while yelling nein. After a little struggle, holding them by the collars, they obeyed my command for some reason to sit and stay. Maybe it was because of the tone of my voice and the fact I spoke in German. Rick quickly stood up.

The other two animals stood there watching what had just happened. Limping, Rick retreated to the porch, sat down, and looked at his leg.

"What happened?" I asked, while standing there holding both dogs by the collar, one in each hand.

"I went to read the name tag and tripped. I fell on him so he attacked me. Then the other one went for my leg. It wasn't their fault. I forgot to use German."

In a stern tone Rick told the two dogs to sit and stay in German. They sat down obeying his commands.

"How's your leg?" I saw it was bleeding a little.

"Not good, but the leather boots saved my foot from some serious bites."

I wrapped my bandanna around his ankle. The wolf dogs were sitting there staring at us. "What do we do now?" I asked.

A dog bite hurts like hell. The teeth are sharp and can easily puncture the skin down to the bone. A German Shepherd has the same bite force as a Pit Bull.

Rick replied, "If they wanted to they could have done a lot more damage to me. We have to get them in the kennels so we can handle them one at a time. Then we'll feed them. After that I gotta go see the Doc."

I watched while Rick commanded the four dogs into the cages. The two that bit him followed his orders. They actually liked going in the kennel. Rick told me that each dog knows which cage is theirs. Once inside they felt safe because it's their home. After they were locked up we gave them food and water. Rick stated the dogs probably come here every night to rest.

We had two males and two females. Adolf and Britta were the oldest. The other dogs, the ones that bit Rick, were Dierk and Freda. As we looked at them Rick said, "I think Freda is pregnant."

"How can you tell?" I asked.

"Her belly is a little larger than it should be."

"How far along is she?"

"Normal gestation is an average of 63 days. I guess she could give birth any day."

"How many pups do they have?"

Rick said, "Usually about four or five."

"Shit, that gives us eight dogs."

Rick scratched his chin and pulled out two smokes. After lighting up we sat there thinking. I said, "It's getting late and you need to see the Doc."

Rick answered, "Yeah, but we can't just leave these dogs locked up here all night."

Thinking for a minute I answered him. "You're right they'd be an easy target for Free Roamers."

"Exactly. We need to make some kennels on Tocabaga before we move them."

"Well, if you can drive, take the truck and leave. Tony can stay here with me. Send Tommy and Mike back with some food. The four of us will guard them tonight. Have some men start making the kennels so we can move the dogs tomorrow."

It was 6 pm when Rick pulled away leaving Tony and me on guard duty. I was a little pissed off about having to stay there all night protecting guard dogs. We walked around the house and went to the kennels. When the dogs saw us they started to bark while wagging their tails.

I asked Tony, "Do you know any German?"

"Yeah, a little. Why?"

"These dogs only understand German."

Lucky for me, I knew some German. My Grandmother, on my mother's side, was German. When I was a little kid she taught me to speak German. Teaching us kids German upset my Dad. He told us to never speak German around him.

Dad was in World War II. He got wounded and was permitted to return back to the States. By

*the time he was better the war was over. Dad didn't
like to talk about the war. I only knew he hated the
Nazis.*

I took Tony around the cages and we talked
to the dogs. Tony was a fast learner and the dogs
seemed to like him. They all came up to the wire
cage and licked our hands, their tails wagging when
we said their names. We gave them all a small piece
of an energy bar.

Tony wanted to let one out. I agreed and let
Adolf out. I didn't have a leash but I didn't need
one. Adolf came out and sat in front of us. We
walked to the back porch and sat down. When we
sat down he laid down next to us.

I took out another energy bar for him to eat.
He looked at it, but didn't move. Finally I said,
"Komm, essen." The big Shepherd came over to me
and smelled the food. Then in one swift move he ate
it in one bite. Adolf was indeed a well-trained dog.
We were becoming friends.

I went in the house to find a hair brush and a
leash leaving Tony alone with the big dog. I was
coming back outside when I heard Adolf bark. I ran
to the back door and saw Tony with Adolf standing
there looking into the woods behind the house.

"What's up?" I asked.

"I don't know. Adolf barked and let out a growl. I think someone or something is back there."

It was dusk and more than an hour had gone by since Rick left. I wondered what the hell was taking so long. I phoned Tommy. "Hey, where are you?"

"I'm at home." he replied.

"Did Rick talk to you?"

"No, I haven't seen Rick. Isn't he with you?"

That's why I never like anyone to travel alone. Murphy's Law states: 'anything that can go wrong will go wrong.'

"Rick left here over an hour ago. Get the Hummer and come to Gulfport. We're at 58th Street and 11th Avenue. Hurry up."

"Roger that. I'll bring Mike along." I hung up.

I called Rick's phone but there was no answer. I tried the radio but there was no reply.

I told Tony, "Something has happened to Rick." Then I raised my M4 and looked through the

FLIR scope. I saw the heat signatures of eight people lurking in the woods.

"Tony, there's eight people back there, about 50 yards away."

Tony looked through his scope. "I see them. What do you wanna do?"

Then I remembered. "Stay here with Adolf while I check out the front door."

Tony replied, "Ok, be careful."

Dashing to the front door I quickly surveyed the situation. There were five men across the street with guns. I needed to kill these guys before they could get any closer. Hiding in the shadows of the doorway, I saw two men on my left. There were two more men standing behind an old car across the street. I had a shot at their chest or heads. One man was in the front of the car.

I figured if I shoot the two behind the car first then I can pick off the guy in the front. After that I'll nail the other two before they run for cover. The distance was only about 100 feet. I had to shoot fast and couldn't miss.

I flicked off my safety and took careful aim at the man nearest the driver's door. I aimed at center mass hoping for a heart shot. I was lucky to have my silencer on which reduced noise and muzzle flash.

Looking through the scope I took a breath and slowly let it out. Then I squeezed the trigger. I fired two shots at each man. I quickly moved from man to man shooting all three before they knew what happened. They all went down.

The two guys on my left looked around trying to see where the shots came from. They dropped to the ground. These dopes didn't even try to run behind the car for cover. The dorks had no idea where I was. They started to crawl away, but didn't get too far. I placed one shot in each of their heads, blowing them apart like a watermelon.

Carefully moving out the door I checked around for any more Free Roamers. There weren't any so I went up to each man and shot them in the head to make sure they wouldn't wake up. I was very careful not to come in contact with their bodies or blood.

Looking at them I wondered who they were and where they came from. Were they part of the horde? Do they have Ebola?

I got on the radio to Tony. "I just killed five Roamers who were sneaking up on us. What's going on back there?"

"So far, nothing."

"I'm gonna stay here and watch the front."

"Ok. Adolf and I are fine."

The sun had just set when it started to rain. I could tell a front was moving in because the wind kicked up out of the northwest. Clouds were blocking the moonlight. The weather turned into a miserable mess.

Maybe the rain would force the people in the woods to leave and seek shelter. I heard a vehicle coming. It was Tommy and Mike. Now we had some man power.

Tommy drove his truck up and parked next to the front porch. I filled him in on the details of what was going down. He saw the five dead guys and said, "I see you already took care of a few."

I asked, "Did you see Rick?"

"No, we didn't see him. I got some more bad news … we saw the horde."

"Where at?"

"They were on 34th Street north of here. It looked like they stopped for the night."

"What were they doing?"

"I don't know, they were too far away to see anything."

"So you came here using 34th Street. Rick must have used Gulf Boulevard to go back to Tocabaga."

"Yeah, that's why we didn't see him," Mike said.

"We need to find Rick. First let's eliminate the guys in the woods behind the house. Maybe they're part of the horde." I said.

"Ok, what do you want us do?" Tommy asked.

"Move the Hummer up to the chain link fence and see if you can get a bead on them with the fifty. When they hear that gun, they'll start running. Maybe we'll kill a few in the process."

"Alright let's do this," Mike replied.

"Don't shoot until I tell you. I'm going to the back yard for a better view."

I moved to the back porch as Tommy drove

the truck up to the fence. I spoke in German as I approached Tony and Adolf. "Good Dog, Adolf." He looked at me and wagged his tail.

"Tony, they still there?"

"Yep. They're just standing there waiting for something."

I told Tony the plan was to terminate the threat using the fifty and then move out to find Rick.

Tony asked, "What about the dogs?"

"We'll have to bring them along."

"Great, I'll take care of them."

Tommy who was 50 feet away said, "We see them. Should we open up?"

"Go ahead," I advised.

Mike opened fire and we could feel the blasts vibrating through the air. I watched using the FLIR scope and saw four of them fall after 50 rounds. The others made a run for it.

Adolf and the other dogs were barking like crazy. I knew the loud bangs from the fifty caliber hurt their ears.

The threat was neutralized. I said, "Let's move out."

We let the dogs out and they followed us. Tommy and Mike were sitting in the truck when I brought the dogs up. I introduced them to the animals before we climbed inside. It was important they at least knew the dogs' names.

I was crammed in the back with the four Shepherds. They just sat there as I spoke to them using what German I knew. Tommy was driving and Mike sat in the gun turret. Tony was riding shotgun. We were speeding down 22nd Avenue heading for Gulf Boulevard which runs the length of St. Pete Beach. We reached the beach but didn't see any sign of Rick.

As we slowly proceeded down the street we spotted a group of people near the old Tower Hotel. It was the same hotel that the BOKO KANG gang occupied at one time. The Chinese Army attacked the gang here not long ago.

Tommy stopped behind some shrubs 100 yards away from them. "What do you wanna do?" he asked.

I could hardly hear him as the rain beat down on the roof of the truck.

We all looked intently at the group of about twenty people. I said, "That might be KANG gang."

Tony said, "Yeah, I think you're right. Maybe they captured Rick."

"Look over there on the right side of the street, by the corner of the building. It's our Hummer," Mike commented.

I dismounted for a better view. Using my night vision binoculars I spied the truck. I stared into the crowd and observed that most had a weapon of some kind. They seemed to be searching for something.

They still hadn't spotted us. It was dark and the rain was pouring down. The group moved off the street seeking shelter inside the hotel. The hotel main lobby was a good 200 feet from the road. I didn't see anyone standing guard.

"That's our truck alright, but where's Rick?" I asked.

Tommy said, "We can't let these guys keep our Hummer. We need to get that truck first and then find Rick. Jack, you dismount and sneak up on the west side of the street. If anyone comes out the front door take them out. We'll drive up to the Hummer and Tony will grab it. Then I'll you pick up."

I interrupted, "What about Rick?"

"Let me finish. Once we got the truck we'll come back and find him."

I didn't like that idea but we had no choice.

"Ok." I opened the back door and ordered Adolf out. He eagerly jumped out into the pouring rain. I told him to heel. I figured the dog could see things and hear things I couldn't. He could be a big help if I got into a bind.

The Shepherd stuck close by my side as we moved to the edge of the street. We had to cover 100 yards. Jogging in a slow trot, I reached a point that offered me a good view of the front door. I was undercover behind some large bushes. The wolf dog was sitting by my side. The rain was starting to subside.

Suddenly Adolf was restless. He got up and started to walk away. I ordered him to stay, but he just turned and looked at me, as if to say follow me. Adolf smelled the ground as he slowly moved toward a clump of over-grown bushes.

I raised my M4 and flicked off the safety. Adolf stuck his head into the bushes and I could see his tail wagging. I thought, *what the hell*? I pushed aside some limbs and bent down staring into the bushes to see what was there.

Rick looked up at me. "What the hell took you so long?"

"Holy crap! You're alive." I stuck out my hand to help him up. He grabbed it and I pulled him up.

Rick said, "I can't walk. I think my ankle's broken."

I got on the radio. "Tommy, bring the Hummer up here; I found Rick. He can't walk."

The truck raced up and Tony jumped out to help me put Rick in the vehicle. Adolf and I jumped inside next to Rick. Tony ran to get the other Humvee about 100 feet away.

We had no sooner jumped in and started the motor when rounds pinged off the bullet proof skin. Mike followed the incoming tracer rounds to the source and opened up on the location with the 50 caliber.

As both trucks sped away a group of men came running out of the hotel firing at us. It was too late because we were out of range. Heading home felt great. We were lucky, very lucky, or maybe it wasn't luck at all thanks to Adolf.

Riding home Adolf was licking Rick's face. Thank God we brought the dogs along. It seemed amazing that the big Shepherd was able to smell Rick in all the rain.

I asked Rick, "Are you shot?"

"Yeah, in my left arm. It's just a flesh wound, but my ankle is killing me."

"What happen?" Mike asked.

"I was driving back and three little kids were in the street. I didn't see anyone else so I stopped to help them. I got out and asked them if they needed food. They backed away from me and started to run. I chased them for a little while, but stopped when I realized I didn't have my gun.

"Like a dummy I left my rifle, phone, and radio in the truck so I turned around to go back. That's when I saw five guys at my truck. It was a trick. They turned their guns on me. I ran like hell as they were shooting and jumped over a wall, landing the wrong way on my ankle."

Britta and Adolf were licking Rick's face like it was a piece of cake. Finally Rick had to tell them nein (no).

Laying there in obvious pain, Rick continued his story. "Anyway, I managed to crawl into the bushes and hide. They came looking for me, but gave up when it started to pour."

"You're one lucky S.O.B.," I told him.

"Yeah, I didn't know what I was gonna do. It looks like Adolf saved my life. It's a good sign. We saved his life and he saved mine."

I hadn't thought about it that way, but Rick was right. We did save the Shepherds lives. They truly are man's best friend.

We rushed Rick to Doc Scott's office. Doc had a lot of work to do on Rick with dog bites, a bullet wound, and a possible broken ankle.

Tony and I had to find a place for the dogs. I suggested why not put them in the jail at the fort for the night. Tony agreed and grabbed some bowls for water. He wanted to stay with the dogs all night.

Tony asked me, "What are we gonna feed them?"

"I suggest some boneless meat of some kind. We feed our little dog strips of chicken and fish mixed with some bread. They pretty much eat what we do. I'll arrange for some food in the morning."

I went back to the Green Room. Mike and Tommy were waiting for me. We had a drink and all agreed that Rick was a lucky guy. If it hadn't been for Adolf he would have been killed for sure.

This reinforced my thinking that we should never go on a mission alone. Even with three warriors you run a risk of getting killed. You never know what's out there. You never know who's trying to kill you. It's not safe on the streets and it hasn't gotten any better in years.

Tommy and I went home but Mike went to visit Lisa. I think that's going to be his new home.

JULY 17, 2025

I woke up and had a cup of coffee while making a list of what needed to be done today. First and foremost we had to make a kennel. We needed to select men who would be the handlers. I had to check how Rick was doing.

First things first, I got on the radio. "Rick, come in."

"Yeah, what's up?"

"How are you doing?"

"Not bad. My ankle isn't broken. It's just sprained, but I can't walk too well."

I replied, "Tony stayed with the dogs in the jail last night. We need to get a kennel built. You got any ideas?"

"We'll build it in the baseball field parking lot. There's a lot of trees there to provide some shade. I'll get Stan on it right away. He made the kennel for my dogs."

"Ok. Thanks, Rick. I'm gonna check on Tony now."

The radio hissed. "I heard you guys talking.

I'm doing fine," Tony said.

"How are the dogs?" I asked.

"Hungry. Could you bring some food for them and me?"

"Ok, I'll be there in about an hour."

While saying good-bye to my wife she commented, "I had a German Shepherd when I was a kid. I loved that dog. Someone broke into our house and killed him when we went to the store."

"I didn't know that. What was its name?"

"His name was Rex. Do you think we could have one of those Shepherds?"

"I don't know, Honey. We have little kids here and these are guard dogs. One of them is going to have puppies in a month. Maybe we can have one of them."

"Why don't you take Johnny and Shanda with you? See how they react to the kids."

"Look, that's not a good idea right now. The dogs are adjusting to a new home."

I walked out the door and drove to Steve's restaurant to pick up some food for the new canine members of Tocabaga. While Steve was preparing the grub, I made a sign-up list for anyone who wanted to be a canine handler. I posted it in the Green Room. I knew Tony would take one dog which meant we needed three more people.

My general plan was to use the dogs for patrols at the fort. These would be roving patrols so the dogs would get plenty of exercise. This would greatly enhance our security in that area.

While I was at the Green Room Chris told me the radar was up and running. So between the dogs and radar we had the eight mile long beach covered. Everything was going as planned.

I jumped in my truck with a 20-pound pot filled with food and drove to the fort. As I pulled up I observed that Tony had the dogs out in the field and was giving them commands. When they spotted the truck they ran over to it barking.

I climbed out and Adolf immediately approached me wagging his tail. He jumped up and put his big front paws on my chest. I pushed him down and petted his head.

I gave the pot to Tony and said, "How they doing?"

"Great … I think. I didn't have any problems." We walked over to the jail where Tony had their bowls lined up two feet apart. Tony told them to sit stay as he spooned out the food. The wolf dogs sat there until Tony gave them the command to eat which is 'essen'. They gobbled up the food quickly and wanted more.

I pulled out a list of German training commands which were also in English. I said, "Every time you use a command in German repeat it in English. That way they'll learn English words."

"Yeah, I've been doing that. I think they already know some English," Tony replied.

"That's good."

"Hey, did you bring me anything to eat?"

"Of course I did." I handed him a plastic bag which contained two fried chicken sandwiches and a few boiled potatoes.

We kept the dogs in the cell while we went to the officer quarters so Tony could eat his breakfast. While he was eating, I laid out my plan for our new friends.

"Tony, I'd like you to be a trainer along with Rick. Rick should be here tomorrow to help out if his ankle is better. The new kennels are being built as we speak."

"That sounds good to me. I like the Shepherds and they like me. What do you want me to do?"

"Right now continue working with the dogs all day. Take one out at a time for a couple of hours and go over the commands in German and English. Basically these dogs are already trained; they just don't know English. I want you to walk them down the beach and all over Fort Desoto. They need to know this island as well as us. After a week of that, take them around Tocabaga to each guard location. Let them meet all our security people."

"How long do you want me to do that?"

"I think in a month they'll be pretty well adjusted to their new home. Freda will be giving birth by then."

Tony took a big bite out of his sandwich and looked at me. "If it's ok I'd like to keep Britta. We kind of bonded for some reason."

"Whatever dog you like is yours. Myself, I like Adolf because he's older and well adjusted."

"Are you gonna keep him?"

"I don't know. My wife wants a Shepherd, but these aren't normal dogs. I'll see what happens. If Adolf can be trusted around my family then maybe I'll keep him."

"Jack, I already made some leashes from some strap I found in the storage area. Let's take Britta and Adolf for a walk on the beach."

Tony and I went for a two hour walk from one end of the beach to the other. The dogs loved it and especially liked going in the salt water. The salt water kills any fleas or ticks that they might have.

Returning to the HQ room, Tony had found a couple of hair brushes. We gave both dogs a much needed soapy shower and brushed them until their coats were smooth. They liked the attention.

I really liked Adolf, but I didn't like his name. I guessed that Adolf was about five years old. He was smart as heck and friendly. Maybe he could fit in with my family. I'd have to discuss it with everyone before making any final decision. Once you take a dog they become part of your family, so you'd better be 100 percent sure.

I spent all day with the dogs and left at 5 pm with Tony to get more food from Steve. I stopped in the Green Room for a quick drink and found Maggie there with Chris. Looking at the posted handler sign, I noticed that both of them had signed up.

Maggie said, "Jack, I really want to be a handler. You know, I love dogs."

"Yep, I know that. I have just the dog for you. Her name is Freda. She's gonna have pups and you're just the person to handle that."

"How soon will she have pups?"

"Any day, as far as we can tell. If you'd, like go down to the fort with Tony and meet her. Tony is picking up some food to take back. He's over at Steve's."

Chris asked, "What about me?"

Years ago Chris had a Jack Russell. Chris knew how to work with dogs. He'd make a perfect handler.

"Oh, I got a dog for you also. Its name is Dierk. Go with Maggie and meet your new dog. Tony has a list of commands written in German and English. Since the dogs only understand German you need to memorize that list. The idea is to teach them English."

"How do we do that?" Maggie inquired.

"Every time you give a command use the English word first, and then the German word after it. In a few weeks try making commands in English only. You both need to remember these aren't normal dogs. They're trained guard dogs."

They both left to find Tony so they could meet their new friends. I needed to make up a training plan so all the handlers would be doing the same routines. I went home to work on that.

As I sat in my office making up a plan, it occurred to me that these Shepherds would be a valuable asset to Tocabaga. Besides guard duty they could help locate missing persons which could be of real benefit in the future. They could also be used for hunting.

I felt good about our new friends. I couldn't wait to see Adolf the next day.

JULY 31, 2025

It's been a couple of weeks since my last entry. There hasn't been much to write about. I haven't heard from Rico, so I assume he's dead. We may never know what happened to him. He was either killed or died of Ebola. It's hard to imagine that anyone could kill Rico. I hate to think about it.

None of my people have been back to his compound fearing that Ebola-infected people may be roaming around the area. We're on lock down and no one is going in or out of Tocabaga unless it's approved. If someone needs to leave the island then a four person security team will accompany them.

We are hoping that no Ebola carriers show up at our door step. Security is on high alert. When dealing with Ebola there are many logistical problems. Suppose a person or even worse a horde of people show up at our bridge. We can't let them in because they may have Ebola or been exposed to it. There's a 10 to 30 day incubation period.

Speaking of the horde we haven't seen them or know where they went since no one has been off Tocabaga for a while.

Another problem with Ebola is you can't

touch anyone or interact with them. The best we can do is give them food, water, and maybe the EVB150 oral vaccine. Then we have to send them on their way.

But what if they don't want to leave? What if they just camp out on our roadway and expect or demand us to give them food and water. What do we do with these poor souls? Do we shoot them and put them out of their misery?

Well there's a problem with shooting them because then we'll have infected bodies lying in the road near our compound. Bodies with Ebola can be contagious for up to 60 days. You can't let the dead just lay there. Coyotes might eat them and become contaminated. They could spread the damn disease to other animals.

That means we have to go out and remove the bodies. If we throw them in the water and the sharks eat them, will they get Ebola? No one knows the answer to that. Would that contaminate our fish food supply? We don't know.

We can't pick them up and bury them because we'll be exposed. The only thing we can do is burn the bodies to kill the virus. Then pick up the ashes and dump them in the water.

Thank God, so far Albert's family hasn't

shown any symptoms of Ebola. I still don't know what to do if they come down with it. Doc was supposed to make a plan to deal with it. Ebola creates a lot of problems.

I made my mind up to add another layer of security. We'll put up a series of chain link 12 foot fences, topped with razor wire, half a mile from the Tocabaga Bridge. Three fences spanning the road will force an enemy to climb them, bash them down, or go around them in the water. There'll be a 40 foot killing zone in between each fence.

My plan is to run the fence along the shoreline all the way back to the bridge. If anyone tries to use the water to bypass the road block they would still have to cut or climb another fence to get on the bridge. This would slow down any intruders and allow us time to pick them off.

Of course, we still have our claymore mines positioned on the guard rails lining the road. There are over 1,000 mines that we can blow which would terminate any horde of unwanted trespassers.

In addition there would be four men stationed at the first fence once completed. They'll be armed with M4's, M249 light machine guns, and hand grenades. A few old cars will serve provide cover from gun fire. One of our bullet-proof Hummers could also be there at night.

These improvements, along with the new radar system, would make our little island a lot safer until the Rangers return. I want to start this new line of security as soon as possible.

The Shepherds are getting along great. They've already learned most of the English command words. The wolf dogs are adjusting very well to their new homes. I decided to adopt Adolf. He's adjusting well to my family. He's friendly to the kids and my wife. I made it clear he wasn't a household pet like our little toy poodle, which he seems indifferent to. They just smell each other and go their own ways. Adolf stays on the patio at night. During the day I take him with me everywhere I go.

The canines are being used for security patrols. They are working out better than I expected. Adolf made everyone at my house feel more secure. He barks when anyone comes around.

A few days ago a chopper flew in and collected the EVB150 from us for distribution to the Military. Captain Sessions called me and advised that the Army had taken over Washington D.C. after a little struggle. The President and his cabinet had been placed under arrest along with most of the Congress. His Rangers were still doing mop operations in the Keys.

That was good news because it means the

country is on the long road to recovery. We're on the road to freedom under the United States Constitution. Yes, it's going to be a long difficult trip to get back to normal. It will take years of hard work, but now there's a light at the end of the tunnel.

During the past few years, thousands of people have been killed or died of starvation. Basically there are very few businesses open to buy products or food. The whole economy is a disaster. The entire nation is still like the Wild West. The rule of law is at the end of a gun. Those with the most guns rule. Gangs and small armies still roam the country looking to take what they want by force.

For now we have to remain vigilant. We have to remain strong. We will continue to fight to stay alive.

AUGUST 1, 2025

The adult members of my family were sitting on the patio talking about what we could do to help establish the new government. We needed to do something for our city and country. The question was what could we do?

What came first, the chicken or the egg? Of course it was the chicken. When we look at our country, what needs to be done first? The answer is simple. We need to establish law and order. We have the laws but not the order. There are no more major law enforcement agencies.

It's necessary to appoint a County Sheriff and enroll as many Deputies as possible. A local police force is required for each city. The problem is how do you do that? There's no money to pay them and when they're on duty their families are unprotected.

There's only one way to solve this problem and that's to use vigilante groups. These are groups of self-appointed citizens, who undertake law enforcement in their community without legal authority, because the legal agencies are inadequate. So in essence, they do become the legal authority as long as they follow the laws on the books. Right or wrong, that's the way I look at it.

I told my family that since martial law has been declared then maybe Captain Sessions could appoint a group to help enforce the rule of law. I decided to discuss this with Sessions as soon as possible. In the meantime we'll do what's necessary to protect ourselves from the forces of evil.

One major problem is that most of our security team doesn't want to ride around and enforce laws all over the city. It's dangerous work so why risk your life when you can stay safe on Tocabaga? Then there's the Ebola factor. Ebola scares the shit out of everyone.

Tommy, Ron, and I went to the Green Room at 5 pm and found Army Mike there along with Lisa and Rick. Somehow the discussion got around to our food supply. Basically we obtain most of our protein from fish, chickens, eggs, and some pork from the wild pigs. Carlos, one of our best hunters, kills one pig every couple of weeks. We don't have many wild pigs at the fort so pork is a rare treat.

Mike said, "It sure would be nice to have some beef or deer meat."

Lisa replied, "Yeah, I'm so sick of fish and chicken."

"I know where we can go deer hunting," Ron commented.

"Where's that?" Mike asked.

"Up north, near my old cabin in the woods, about 10 miles from Bushnell City."

I responded, "It's a two-hour drive on the Interstate. There's wild cattle, deer, and turkeys all over the place."

"Yep, and even gators if you want any," Ron stated.

"It's a dangerous trip into no-man's-land. We have no idea what's up there," Tommy said.

"There's only good old boys and rednecks up there. I think it'll be safe. We just tell them we're there to hunt a few deer. It's probably safer than going to St. Petersburg," Ron replied.

Mike said, "I'm willing to go."

I looked around the room and everyone was nodding their head in agreement. I took a drink and pulled out a smoke. Mike lit it for me and said, "Come on big guy. Are you afraid of a few good old boys?"

I took a drag and replied, "No, it's the

inbred idiots who don't even know what day it is. They don't have a full deck. Those are the ones that'll kill you."

Ron asked, "Well, are we going or not? It's up to you, Jack."

"Ok, but we need the two Hummers for security and one big F 350 pick-up to carry the meat. I wanna bring along Carlos because he's our best hunter. The crew will be Ron, Mike, Tommy, Carlos, and Rick. We'll need a total of eight people."

"Hey, what about me?" Lisa asked.

"If you wanna come along, fine." Lisa let out a big smile and blew me a kiss. "We need one more man," I said.

Just then Maggie walked in the bar. Everyone looked at her and she said, "What? What's everyone looking at me for?" Maggie went behind the bar and poured herself a shot of Wild Turkey.

She had Freda with her so Adolf went to greet her. I was pretty sure that Freda was Adolf's daughter. Freda still hadn't given birth. The Shepherds were playing with each other.

I replied, "You wanna go on a hunt?"

"A hunt for what?" Maggie asked.

"We're going on a deer hunt."

Maggie slammed down her shot glass. "Shit yeah, count me in."

I looked at Tommy. "Do you wanna bring along Johnny and teach him how to hunt?"

"I don't know, let me think about that."

"Ok, we take off at 8 am. Everyone meet at the bridge. This is going to be an all-day trip." We all had a few more drinks and went home.

I was excited about the hunt because we hadn't had a real steak for a long time. If we could kill three cows, and a couple of deer, that would more than feed everyone on Tocabaga for a few weeks. I could taste that big juicy steak as I fell asleep.

AUGUST 2, 2025

It was a bright sunny day as I loaded the truck with all our gear. It should be like a Sunday drive out in the country.

I remember in the good old days my father would take the whole family for a Sunday drive. It was a big deal to drive out into the country side. We'd leave the big city and head out into the wide open spaces of the country.

I used to wonder in amazement at how farmers lived. I always thought it would be a great lifestyle. Being a farmer is a lot of hard work, but you have a lot of freedom.

Tommy showed up with little Johnny. "Johnny's coming along. He's gotta learn how to hunt sometime."

I rubbed Johnny on the head. "It's gonna be fun. Just listen to your Dad and me."

Jim Bo was staying behind to watch the family instead of Ron. He would also take care of

Maggie's dog, Freda, while she was gone. Jim helped us finish loading the gear and asked me, "What route are you taking?"

"Interstate 75 to the Bushnell exit."

In the old days we had all been to Ron's cabin many times. We knew there were two routes you could take to get there. I picked the one that was the most direct.

We double checked all the gear and rolled out. Tommy, Johnny, and I, along with Adolf were in the first Hummer. Ron was driving the second Humvee with Mike, Lisa, and Maggie. Last in the convoy was the F-350 truck with Carlos and Rick.

The most dangerous part of our route took us through the northeast side of Tampa. We kept the 50 calibers manned while passing through Tampa in case some dirt-bags tried to jump us.

As we drove along with our little American Flags flapping in the wind, we saw a few cars and some people walking on the side of the highway. They looked at us and some of them waved. We waved back as if they were friends. Some of them gave us the finger and we gave it back. We passed the danger zone with no problems and were soon out in the countryside.

We were cruising along at 45 mph. All we could hear was the rumble of the big knobby off-road tires. It was almost 10 am and sweat was dripping off my head. I was stuffed in the back seat with Adolf. His long tongue was hanging out trying to stay cool.

Johnny said, "I gotta pee."

I replied, "Me, too. Pull over here."

Tommy pulled over to the side of the road and the Hummer rumbled to a stop. The other trucks pulled up behind us. I couldn't wait to get out and neither could Adolf.

I opened the door and Adolf jumped out. He ran to the grass along with Johnny. They both sat down in the shade of a big tree. I joined them. It felt cool there because of a slight breeze.

Tommy broke out some water and snacks for everyone. It was peaceful except for a passing car or truck every now and then. I peered out into the wide open field of high grass. It seemed strange not seeing a single house or building.

Rick said, "This is nice. I wish I had a little house right out there in the middle."

"It reminds me of my Dad's farm. Big open fields are so peaceful," Mike commented, who was sitting in the gun turret keeping watch.

The high grass waved back and forth creating a hypnotic-like spell. We just sat there looking at that dumb field. We were relaxed for the first time in a long time. The sense of danger had been lifted off our shoulders by Mother Nature.

I pulled a piece of grass out of the ground, stuck it in my mouth, and chewed on it. I used to do that when I was a kid. It triggered memories from long ago. Grass actually has very little taste. It tasted green to me, like a plant should.

We were suddenly brought back to the real world by the sound of trucks. Mike yelled, "We got company, there's 20 vehicles moving south, on the other side of the highway."

Everyone stood up including our guard dog. Tommy moved quickly to the Hummer machine gun as the trucks came to a stop directly across from us.

I said, "Johnny, get in the truck with your Dad." Everyone moved to their vehicles for protection.

I scanned the entire line of trucks and estimated there were about 150 people in all. Two men came walking across the median carrying a white flag along with rifles. Stopping about 50 feet away they shouted, "We mean you no harm. We just want some information. Can we come over?"

I yelled, "You can come on over but leave your guns there!"

I stepped out from behind the truck as the two heavy-set men came walking up. Adolf was by my side and he growled as they approached. I told him heel, stay. They looked at the dog and slowly held out their hands for me to shake from a few feet away.

I responded, "I'm Jack Gunn. Sorry, we don't shake hands because of Ebola." Adolf sat there growling at the strangers.

"It's nice to meet you. My name is Sam Smith and this is Daniel Gibbs. We're the leaders of this convoy. I can assure you we don't have Ebola." He spoke in a firm tone, as he glanced down at the dog.

I looked at them closely. They were well-dressed, wearing jeans and clean shirts. They had short hair and were clean shaven. I asked, "Where are you headed?"

Sam said, "We're going as far south as possible."

I could tell by his accent he was from up north; probably from somewhere in the mid-west. "Where are you from?"

Sam reached out to pet Adolf and he showed his teeth. I warned him, "He'll bite you." Sam quickly pulled his hand back.

"We're from Cleveland," Daniel answered. "Where are you guys from?"

I said, "South of here, about 50 miles." I didn't wanna tell them exactly where.

"How many are in your group back there?" Daniel asked.

"We have about 600 people."

"Why are you guys heading north?" Sam asked.

Tommy standing in the gun turret replied, "We're going hunting."

I advised them, "We saw a horde of people a few days ago heading south. There was about a thousand of them. What's going on? Why are all you people moving south?"

"We're headed south because of global cooling and the Arctic Vortex." Daniel said.

"Yeah, we heard about the cooling, but we don't know much about it."

"Well, July and August are usually the hottest months. A week ago we had snow. So we're getting out of there while we can. It's going to be a really bad winter."

Sam butted in, "There isn't gonna be any food. All the crops were ruined by the freeze."

I looked at them sweating in the bright sun and said, "Let's sit over there in the shade."

As we walked by the Humvee Sam ran his hand over the hood and said, "This is a weapon we could use in our convoy." He stood there gazing at the machine gun.

We moved under the tree, out of sight of his men, behind our trucks and sat down. Adolf heeled and sat next to me.

"Are you guys in the Army?"

"No, we're not the Army."

I looked around and noted that Tommy and Mike kept watch on the group across the highway from the gun turrets.

Daniel commented, "If you're not in the

Army where'd you get all the gear and automatic weapons from?"

I replied, "From friends in the Army." That's all I wanted to tell them.

"Where are your Army friends?"

"That's classified information."

"Ok, fair enough. Can you tell us what's between here and Tampa?" Sam inquired, as he gazed at my weapons and Black Bear knife.

"Not much, just a few Free Roamers here and there."

"That's a hell of a good looking knife on your vest. Can I see it?" Sam said.

"No one touches my knife."

He nodded his head. "I know how you feel. I like knives, too." I noticed there was a big Gerber Bowie hanging on his belt.

Just then Maggie and Lisa came over to the tree and sat down next to me. Sam asked, "Are these your daughters?"

It wasn't any of his business who they were and I resented his question. Maggie sitting Indian style, holding her M4 between her crossed legs, replied, "No, we're his women. Why do you wanna know?"

"Just curious, that's all. You're good looking women wearing some pretty fancy uniforms. Do you know how to use those guns?"

In a sarcastic tone Lisa responded, "Do you wanna find out?"

Daniel jumped in the conversation. "Sam didn't mean anything. It's just that you don't see good looking women dressed in combat gear every day."

The two men were just about drooling while gawking at the girls. They were beautiful and cute, sitting there holding big guns, with their hair up in pig tails. They didn't look dangerous, but these guys had no idea.

I asked in a firm tone, "Ok, what do you really want?"

"Well, we could use some fuel and food supplies. Why don't we go hunting with you?"

"Sorry, we can't do that."

"Why not?" Sam asked, glaring at the girls like a hungry wolf.

I looked at Sam and then at Daniel. "It's our hunting grounds, that's why."

I thought these guys were up to no good. They didn't want food. They wanted our guns and women. After talking to someone for a few minutes I can smell if their good or bad. My sixth sense was telling me ... Danger.

"Ok, then just help us out and tell us where we can get some food, guns, and ammo around here," Sam said.

Maggie leaned in towards him. "We can't tell you shit, Mister. We don't know who the hell you are."

"We're just people trying to get along," Daniel replied.

"No need to get your panties in a knot," Sam said. "Jack, what do you think?"

I petted Adolf and stood up. Adolf stood up at the same time. "I think we've wasted enough time talking."

Sam looked up at me and replied, "Now

hold on there, we don't mean you any harm. There's no need to be afraid of us just because we out number you. I'll tell you what we'll do. We'll pay you in gold for your Hummers' and some extra for the women. You can keep the pick-up truck."

I responded, "First of all, we're not afraid of you, asshole. The second thing is, you can't buy our women." He made a big mistake offering to buy the girls. Now I knew he was a dirt-bag for sure.

Sam stood up and put his hand on his Bowie knife. Adolf let out a low growl, warning him to watch his step. Maggie and Lisa stood up with their guns in low ready position. Daniel stood up with a disappointed look on his face and threw his hands in the air in disgust.

Sam spoke up. "You know what I think? I think you don't have any other people. You and your family are just trying to survive like we are. Why don't you join us and share what you have. A big group like ours is safer for the women."

I quickly racked a round into my M4 and flipped off the safety. "Talking is over now."

Sam and Daniel both looked at me. I saw Sam starting to reach behind his back. I pointed my M4 at him and said, "You'll be dead before you get that gun out."

Sam replied, "All I gotta do is yell for help and my men will gun you down."

"You stupid piece of shit, you do that and you're dead. I won't hesitate to kill you both. Put your hands up!"

"I don't think you have the guts to do that."

Maggie laughed. "Don't bet your life on that." She rammed her gun barrel into his fat belly knocking the wind out of him. "Jack, let me kill him."

I said, "Maggie get their guns. Then zip-tie their hands behind their backs and do their feet also. Gag these guys so they can't yell."

Maggie pulled the guns out of their belts. "Hey, look at these little pea shooters." Both had little derringers which made Maggie and Lisa laugh.

Lisa said, "Cute little pop guns. We're keeping these."

Sam protested, "Hey, come on now!"

I bashed him in the face with the barrel of my gun. Blood flowed out of the corner of his mouth as he fell to the ground. Adolf grabbed hold of Sam's leg. I had to pull him off. I reached down and took Sam's Bowie. Daniel didn't move a muscle. I could tell he was scared.

Lisa and Maggie zip-tied them up and stuffed rags in their mouths. They knocked Daniel to the ground. He grunted as his face smashed into the dirt.

Maggie said, "I'll slice one of their Achilles so they can't walk away."

I replied, "Go ahead."

The dorks were whining like little babies as Maggie pulled out her machete. Maggie yelled, "Stop crying you little bitches! Don't move or I could slip and cut off your foot." She sliced the tendons like a trained surgeon. The gag reduced their screams to a muffled cry of pain.

With wide eyes they watched me take a hand grenade out. I told Lisa, "Go to the truck and get some fishing line."

I tied the monofilament line to the pin and then tied the other end to Sam's belt. I carefully placed the grenade underneath Daniel leaving about ten inches of slack. I covered the line with dirt.

I guessed Sam's men would pick him up first since he was the boss. I left a little booby trap for his men. I figured that when his men come running over and help him up … KABOOM.

I warned them, "Don't move a muscle or this will blow you to shit."

Lisa giggled and said, "Great idea, Jack."

I told my crew to mount up and we roared out with the pedals to the metal. My crew machine gunned the convoy of trucks, as much as possible, while we drove away at a high rate of speed.

Have you ever seen what a 50 caliber machine gun can do? Our two guns blew the shit out of the convoy in a few minutes. The men in the convoy didn't know what hit them as they all scampered for cover. They never had a chance to return fire.

I can only imagine what happen to Sam and Daniel. The poor bastards learned a lesson the hard way. It really pissed me off that they tried to buy Maggie and Lisa. I know if the dorks had the chance, they would have killed us. They bit off more than they could chew.

We continued down I-75 and observed a few cars along the way that were burning on the side of the road. Next to the cars were dead bodies which told me that Sam's convoy was most likely responsible for those dirty deeds. We didn't stop because it was too dangerous.

We arrived at the Bushnell exit. Our group would follow Route 48 west for about 10 miles to Trails End Road. Trails End Road is where Ron's cabin was located. It was deep in the woods at the end of the trail, just like the name says. There's three ways to get there. One is by truck, another is by boat from the river, and the third is through the swamp on foot.

The cabin is located on a dry patch of land in the middle of the swamp. On the west side is a river that runs all the way to the Gulf of Mexico. The only road in is Trails End.

I never liked the name Trails End Road. It reminded me of an old western movie where the cowboy's buddy is shot and dying. With his last breath he says, 'It's the End of the Trail for me partner.'

No one hikes through the swamp which is infested with bears, snakes, gators, Florida panthers, and who knows what else. The area is pretty secure from outsiders. There are a few people that live back there. Ron calls them good old boys. He knows them all because he lived there for years until the collapse.

After traveling about three miles down Trails End Road, we spotted a couple of wild cattle and a few turkeys. We pulled over to the side of the road and jumped out. The animals didn't even notice our presence.

Carlos asked, "Ron, can we shoot those?"

"Yeah, I don't see why not. No one lives here anymore."

Carlos grabbed his shotgun and Tommy picked up his 308. Tommy told Carlos, "I'll pick off the cows from here." They were about 300 yards away.

Carlos replied, "I'll get the turkeys." Carlos trekked out across the open field after the wild turkeys.

The closer Carlos got to the turkeys they would keep moving away from him. We all started to laugh. The turkeys were smart enough to keep a safe distance from Carlos.

Tommy said, "I'm gonna shoot these cows before they move too far away."

Tommy directed Johnny to watch him set up the gun for the kill. It was an easy shot for him. He folded down his bipod, placed it on the hood of the truck, and took aim explaining everything he was doing to his son.

The 308 thundered out and echoed across the field. With two shots he had two kills. The cattle just stood there as each one fell to the ground. They didn't run or even look around.

We all turned to see what Carlos was up to. He was out of sight. Rick said, "I'll go find him." He jumped into the F-350 and drove out in the field.

I got on the radio. "Carlos, come in."

Rick answered, "Carlos left his radio in the truck."

"That dumb shit."

"Yeah, he's headed for the woods. I'll try to catch him before he gets there. The problem is I can't go too fast because there's so many big ruts and holes."

"Take it easy and don't break an axle. We need that truck to haul back the meat," I advised.

"I can see him. He's running into the swamp after those damn turkeys." I heard Rick beeping the truck horn over the radio.

I looked at Tommy and said, "Carlos is chasing the damn turkeys into the woods."

"The fool should just let them go. We'll see more of them. We need to load up the cattle before some coyotes come along," Tommy said.

"Go ahead over there and watch them. Take Maggie and Lisa with you. We'll go search for Carlos."

Damn it anyhow, something always happens. People need to use their brains. We're in dangerous territory and don't know what or who is out there.

Mike, Ron, and I along with Adolf headed off to the swampy woods to find Carlos. It was a good half mile away. Rick was right; the field was full of big ruts probably caused by wild pigs. Even in the Hummer it was a slow bumpy ride. I could almost walk faster.

Pulling up next to Rick on the edge of the swamp, I asked, "Which way did he go?"

Rick said, "I'm not sure. He went in the woods right here," pointing to a path directly in front of his truck.

We stood there peering into the thickly

wooded swamp. Even though it was daylight, the swamp with its big Spanish Moss covered trees was dark, very dark. It was a foreboding force that wasn't inviting. It looked dangerous and I knew it was. I, for one, didn't want to enter the darkness.

Spanish moss is a plant that grows on larger trees. It is commonly found on Oak or Cypress trees in the southeastern United States. It grows as silvery-green festoons hanging down from the tree branches.

I suggested that Rick take his truck and help Tommy field dress the cattle and load them up while we search for Carlos.

Field dressing is the process of removing the internal organs which is necessary to preserve the meat. It must be done as soon as possible to prevent bacteria from growing on the surface of the carcass.

Mike asked, "Are we going in after him?"

I replied, "Shit, we don't even know which way he went."

"Use the dog and track him," Ron said.

"No, I don't wanna use the dog because I don't know what he'll do. Let's fire off a round or two so Carlos can hear us."

"Ok," Mike said.

Mike fired two rounds into the air. A minute or two later we heard two rounds definitely fired from a shotgun. We replied with two more. Then we heard five rounds which sounded somewhat closer, but it was hard to tell.

I fired two more rounds. I heard a faint voice yelling. It was Carlos. I yelled back, "Carlos over here!" Adolf was barking while we all were yelling. It was almost like Adolf was trying to help us. His bark was a lot louder than our yells.

Mike shouted, "This way Carlos!" He fired two more rounds in the air.

I raised my M4 and looked into the dark swamp with my night scope. I scanned for a heat signature. "I see him. He's coming this way."

I kept watching him to make sure he was heading in the right direction. It's easy to get lost in the swamp. As I watched, he would disappear every now and then behind a tree or bush. Mike fired two more rounds.

I said, "What the hell?"

Mike asked, "What?" He also raised his scope to look.

"Someone's chasing Carlos. They're right behind him."

Ron said, "Maybe they're good old boys or swamp people."

Mike replied, "I don't see anyone."

I didn't answer him as I watched two men flank Carlos. One grabbed his arm. They didn't look like normal men. They were very large compared to Carlos who stood almost six foot tall.

I saw a muzzle flash and ... heard the shot. One of the big men fell, letting Carlos go. I estimated he was about 100 yards away. I said, "Mike, look about 100 yards straight into the woods."

I flicked off my safety and took aim at a guy right behind Carlos. I couldn't fire because Carlos was in the way. Carlos tripped and fell giving me an open shot. I fired and the big man stopped. I watched him sit down and counted five other heat signatures come to his aid.

Carlos came stumbling out of the swamp out of breath. Ron helped him up as he fell to the ground. Carlos yelled, "Let's get the hell ... out of here!"

Climbing into the Hummer I asked, "Who are those guys?"

Adolf was peering into the dark woods barking and growling at whatever was there. I had to grab him by the collar and forced him into the back of the Hummer.

Staring at the woods with wide open eyes Carlos yelled, "Come on. Move it! They're coming!"

Mike started the motor and we drove away over the rutted field. We were about 200 yards out and I asked Carlos again, "Were those swamp people?"

Carlos said, "They weren't people. They're animals."

"Animals don't walk on two legs," Mike said.

"This kind does. You ever heard of Skunk Apes?"

I asked, "You mean Bigfoot?"

Ron commented, "There's a lot stories about Skunk Apes being around here."

Carlos continued, "Yeah, I stumbled on a camp of Bigfoots. I was chasing the turkeys, being real quiet, sneaking up on them. I was about 50 feet away from one when I heard your gun fire. The Apes heard it also and jumped out from behind the trees. I saw them and started to run. They came after me. I shot at them but they didn't stop. I didn't have time to reload because I was running. They're faster than hell."

"I don't believe in Bigfoot," Mike said.

"Well I do. There's too much evidence that they exist," I said. Mike looked at me and shook his head.

"So, you weren't lost," Mike said.

Carlos replied, "I wasn't lost. I knew the way back, but if you guys hadn't fired those rounds I would have walked right into their trap."

"Trap? You think they set a trap for you?"

"Not for me, but for the turkeys. I am sure of it." Carlos turned around to look behind us. "Stop! Look, there they are."

Mike stopped and we peered back to the edge of the swamp. They were standing in the shadows of the trees. There was a group of about ten figures. It was too dark to make them out clearly. They stood there not moving, but they were watching us closely. It sent a chill down my spine.

Adolf looked also and growled. Maybe he could smell them.

Mike commented, "That's not proof of Bigfoot. We can't tell what they are from here."

I said, "I don't know if those are Skunk Apes or not but let's get going. We're running out of time."

Carlos replied, "I'm a hunter, I know what I saw. One of them had me by the arm. Look he tore my sleeve off when I tried to get away. They smelled really bad. They were Skunk Apes alright."

Mike laughed, "Ok, whatever you say."

I replied, "Carlos, I believe you."

Mike rubbed it in. "Those are swamp people and that's why they smell bad. If you took a shower once a year you'd smell bad too." Mike let out another loud laugh as we drove away.

Carlos kept looking behind us watching the ape men. I looked back once more only to see them fade away into the darkness of the swamp.

We drove over to Tommy and the rest of the

crew. We told them about the Skunk Apes but no one seemed concerned. They didn't really believe the story.

All of us helped quarter the meat. We cut it up into pieces that would fit into our body bags to keep it clean. It took us a good two hours. We made a real mess of it. Steve should have come along since he knows how to butcher a cow.

With blood all over us Ron said, "Ok, let's go to my cabin and clean up. It'll be getting dark soon so we'll stay the night."

"Good idea," I commented.

A few more miles down the road we crossed the little bridge which brought us to the end of the trail. Ron's cabin, which he built himself, was sitting there looking the same as it did ten years ago. Scattered around the area were a few old trailers and two other hunting cabins.

The cabin sat on a patch of high ground a quarter mile wide and half a mile long. It was surrounded by the swamp. Big Oak and Cypress trees block out the sun. It was ten degrees cooler in the shade. It smelled like the swamp and looked eerie with Spanish Moss hanging off every tree limb.

We dismounted and Ron started the generator. He turned on the propane to heat the hot water tank. Ron's cabin was entirely self-sufficient. There was a septic system along with a fresh water well. The only problem is you need to boil the water before drinking it. I planned on taking a hot shower.

Tommy and Johnny went over to the fire pit and started building a fire which would help keep the mosquitoes at bay. The mosquito is the Florida State bird.

Maggie and Lisa went into the cabin with Ron. They would be the first ones to shower and clean up before we cooked dinner. Mike unzipped one of the body bags. Rick pulled out a nice piece of meat. He plopped it on a cutting board table and began to slice it up into strips. We were going to have fresh beef tonight. The last time we had beef was a while ago when the Rangers provided us a steak dinner.

Ron helped Lisa and Maggie set the table. We were all hungry because the last time we had anything to eat was around 10 o'clock. Adolf was walking around the camp with Johnny getting familiar with the area.

Ron said, "When it gets dark you need to keep him on a leash."

"Why?" I asked.

"At night the gators come out. They'll smell the blood and come over here. They could go after your dog. I lost one that way."

I called Adolf over and commanded him to sit. He smelled the meat and wanted something to eat. All animals have an amazing sense of smell.

Maggie asked, "Will gators come by the fire?"

Ron answered, "Yeah. Gators aren't afraid of anything."

"Then we'll have to shoot them," Lisa replied, with a giggle.

"I'll be in the cabin asleep by then," Ron told her. "I don't wanna mess with any gators."

I said, "We'll keep the meat in the truck so they can't get at it."

"The fire is ready. Let's clean up and eat!" Tommy shouted.

We took our turns in the shower and put on some spare clothes that Ron had kept at the cabin. Ron brought out some cans of baked beans which would go great with the beef steaks. The cans were way past the expiratory date. I opened a can, smelled it, and took a taste. The beans tasted fine to me. I don't think canned beans ever go bad because of all the sugar.

While Mike and Rick were cooking our food I said, "I'd like two men on guard all night. We'll rotate shifts every two hours. Who wants to go first?"

Maggie and Lisa raised their hands to pull first duty starting at 10 pm. Then Adolf, Carlos, and I, followed by Rick and Mike, with Tommy and Ron last. We'd let Johnny sleep the whole night.

Carlos asked, "What if the ape men come after us?"

"I've never seen ape men here. Besides that they're five miles away. They don't know we're here," Ron told him.

I pulled a piece of rare meat off the fire, let it cool a little, and tossed it to Adolf. He gobbled it down in one bite and sat up waiting for more.

After eating the best meal in a long time, Ron and I went for a walk around the camp. It was dusk and soon the swamp would be black. Even a full moon wouldn't shine through the dense tree canopy.

As we were walking back to the cabin Ron commented, "I wonder what happened to the good old boys that lived here."

"Maybe they all left like you did."

Ron shrugged his shoulders. "Yeah, maybe."

I stopped to light up a smoke. Adolf was by my side and he let out a low, soft growl. It's the type of growl that's warning you someone or something is nearby. He pointed directly into the thick woods.

I told Ron, "He smells something."

"He probably smells a gator or something."

I stomped out my butt and looked in the direction that Adolf was pointing. The woods are scary-looking because they're so dark. Anything could be out there. It could be 50 feet away and you wouldn't even see it.

Ron said, "I don't see anything."

"Me neither. Let's go back to the cabin," I replied.

"I got a bottle of JD back at the cabin."

"Great, I could use a good drink."

We were walking away but Adolf still stood there growling. I had to lower my voice and command him to come. It took several verbal commands before he ran to my side. That meant there was something out there for sure. I trusted Adolf's senses more than my own.

Arriving back at the cabin I sat down at the fire and Ron brought out the bottle. Mike took a swig and asked, "Did you guys see any Bigfoots out there?"

I didn't reply and Carlos looked at me. "Well did you see anything, Jack?"

I could tell Carlos was still spooked. "Adolf saw or smelled something but I didn't see anything."

Mike let out a laugh, "I'll believe in Bigfoot when I see him right in front of me."

"Be careful what you ask for," Carlos said.

Ron took a drink, passed the bottle back to me, and commented, "I told you there are swamp people out there."

Maggie said, "All this talk about gators, swamp people, ape men, and Bigfoot is bull shit. You guys are just trying to scare us."

"Yeah, you're trying to frighten us and little Johnny, so cut it out," Lisa said.

Tommy asked Johnny, "Are you scared?"

"No, I'm not afraid of Bigfoot." Johnny jumped and looked around behind him. Everyone laughed but Johnny. "That's not funny." Mike had thrown a stick behind Johnny. He ran over and lightly punched Mike in the arm.

It was almost 10 pm so the men went in the cabin for some much needed rest. I advised Lisa and Maggie to sit in the Hummer during guard duty just in case any gators came around. I would catch about 2 hours of sleep before it was my turn.

AUGUST 3, 2025

SOMETIME AFTER MIDNIGHT

Adolf's low growl woke me up. Soft deep voices were coming from behind the cabin near the swamp. They slowly moved around to the front where the fire circle and trucks were.

I peeked out the window and there were five men walking up to the vehicles. I checked my watch and it was past midnight. I wondered why Maggie and Lisa hadn't called out.

Then I heard a scream. "Jack!" It woke everyone up and my dog started to bark.

Ron asked, "What's going on?"

"There's some men outside," I told him.

Ron gazed out the window and shouted, "It's the swamp people! Don't shoot them!" Ron bolted out the door to greet them. We followed him with our guns in hand. I put Adolf on a leash.

The men were dressed in rubber wading boots, jeans, T-shirts, and had on straw hats. They carried old lever-action rifles and a couple of double-barreled shotguns. They all had long scraggly hair and beards. They turned and watched us come out of the cabin while holding their guns in a ready position.

I immediately wondered if these were the men who chased Carlos. If they were we could be in for a fight because I shot one of them. I looked at Carlos to see his facial expression. He didn't seem concerned about the strange men.

We spread out behind Ron, who greeted them by shaking hands with each one like he was a long lost friend. Ron said, "Greetings friends. I'd like you to meet my family." Ron pointed to us and then to Maggie and Lisa in the truck. The men all nodded their heads as if to say howdy, but none spoke. We all nodded back.

"How can I help you?" Ron asked.

One big brute, stepped forward and spoke up. "We know you many years. What you here for?"

Ron replied, "We came to hunt."

"What you hunt?"

"Wild cattle, deer, and maybe a turkey."

The big man nodded his head and spoke in another language to his men. It sounded like half

English and Spanish. He asked, "You no hunt gators?"

"No hunt gators," Ron replied.

"That good," he replied. He walked over to the pick-up truck and touched a body bag. "You got meat here. Give me some friend."

We all stood there and wondered how much of our meat he was going to take. I knew we could kill these guys, but there was no sense in doing that if we didn't need to. There could be another hundred of them hiding in the swamp. We might not make it out of here alive.

Ron said, "Friend, take what you like."

The big brute ordered two men, to grab some meat out of the truck. They each picked up a bag, which were about 100 pounds each, and carried it over to a small flat-bottom boat. Laying in the bottom of the boat I noticed a dead gator. I assumed they dragged that little boat through the swamp behind them.

A young man said, "Look at them guns, Daddy."

The kid walked over to me and reached out to touch my gun. Adolf growled at him and he backed off.

The kid replied, "I wanna see it," while holding out his hand.

Ron said, "Sorry friend, we don't give our guns away."

The old man whom he called Daddy said, "Leave them be, boy."

I said, "Wait a minute. I got something you'll like."

I went to the Hummer and found the Bowie knife I took from Sam. While there I whispered to Maggie and Lisa to stay in the truck.

If the swamp men get a good look at the girls they might want them for breeding. We've been through that before.

I walked back over to the boy. "Here, you can have this Bowie knife."

His Daddy stepped over to see it. "That a fine knife. Take it, boy."

He reached out and took it from my hand and a smile came across his face. He said, "Thanks, Mister."

Big Daddy asked, "When y'all leave?"

"At day-break," Ron replied.

"Y'all be careful. Swamp Monkeys are about. They don't cotton to strangers." Big Daddy turned and trudged away. His men followed him dragging the small boat back into the swamp. No one said another word.

We watched them disappear into the woods. We saw other shadowy figures come out from behind the trees leaving with them. I was right; there were a bunch of people hidden in the swamp.

Ron said, "I'm glad they're gone."

"Yeah, that was intense," I replied.

"They're simple honest people. They never stole anything from me. If they wanted to they could have broken into my cabin, but they never have."

"Where do they live?" Mike asked.

Ron answered, "I don't know. Rumor is they have a little village somewhere deep in the swamp. The swamp is a big area that covers a couple hundred square miles."

"Screw that, who cares where they live. Did you hear what he said? There's Monkey Men out there," Carlos blurted out.

"Yeah, he must mean Skunk Apes," Mike

said with a slight laugh.

"I don't think it's funny, Mike!" Maggie shouted.

I looked at my watch and it was going on 2 am. I told everyone, "There's no way we're going back to sleep. If everyone agrees, let's load up and move out."

"Monkey Men or Skunk Apes, I don't wanna be around if they come here," Carlos replied.

Everyone started to collect their gear and load it up. Adolf and I were standing by the Hummer as I was having a smoke. Suddenly he let out a low growl. He was tied to the bumper, otherwise he would have took off after whatever was out there.

I looked at him and he was sniffing the air. He smelled something. Putting out my butt, I sniffed the air also. I could smell something and it didn't smell good. I don't know how to describe it, other than it smelled like a wet dog, mixed in with the smell of rotten fish.

I glanced around the woods and looked down the road. I didn't see anything but Adolf kept growling. My sixth sense kicked in. A danger alert went off in my brain.

I yelled, "Hurry up guys! I think we got company coming." I picked up my M4 and scanned all around the camp as everyone was rushing to put their gear in the trucks.

Lisa asked, "Do you see anyone?"

"No, but I can smell something."

Lisa took a big whiff of air. "That smells like shit."

Carlos softly said, "That's them. That's what the apes smell like," as he looked around in the dark clutching his shotgun.

"If we see any Apes don't shoot them. They're an endangered species," Ron commented.

Maggie asked, "What if they attack us?"

I said, "Don't shoot them unless they attack us. Come on people. Let's move it and get out of here." I had no sooner said that and my dog went nuts growling and barking while tugging at the leash.

I turned glancing in the direction he was looking. On the dirt road behind us, shadows appeared out of the foggy mist, about 300 feet away. They seemed like ghosts coming out of the fog one at a time. I shined my Sure Fire flash light at the group but I only saw their red glowing eyes. The fog reflected the light beam obstructing most of my view.

"Here they are!" I yelled. My crew all looked at the shadowy figures with red eyes.

Mike commented, "Holy shit!"

Tommy ushered little Johnny into the Hummer. Just then one of them let out a loud bloodcurdling howl that would scare anyone. Then the others followed in suit. Adolf stopped barking and tucked his tail between his legs as he scampered closer to me.

Maggie asked, "What do they want with us?"

Carlos said, "They want what all animals want, food. They smelled our meat and came to get it."

Ron said, "All right, let's unload the meat." I watched the Bigfoots while Carlos, Ron, and Mike unzipped the bags and threw the meat out onto the road.

The ape men stood there watching what we were doing. We had unloaded about half of the meat when they started to slowly advance. I shouted, "Ok, that's enough! Let's get the hell out of here!"

Everyone scrambled into the vehicles. I did a double check to make sure no one was left behind. We drove across the little bridge stopping about 400 feet away for one last look-see. We never did obtain a good clear view of the mysterious creatures but I think we're all believers now, including Mike.

A big monster, at the head of the pack, reached the pile of meat first. He picked up a big chunk, smelled it, and took a bite. Then he did something strange. He howled and raised his arms in the air. Maybe it was a victory sign they use. Maybe it was a thank you sign. I didn't have any idea what his actions really meant, but I liked to think we did communicate in some way. Maybe we did something good for the poor bastards.

After his actions the rest of the pack moved to the pile of meat and began to feed. We quickly drove away along the fog-lined road. The mist made it tricky driving on Trails End but we made it back to Route 48 with no problems.

We pulled over, stopping in a church parking lot, a few miles away. Everyone dismounted and Carlos said, "See Mike, I told you Skunk Apes were real."

Mike replied, "Yeah, you were right Carlos. If I hadn't seen them with my own eyes I wouldn't have believed it." Mike gave Carlos a little slap on the back as gesture of friendship.

"Yep, we saw Bigfoots. It was an incredible sight," Tommy commented.

"Gee whiz. I didn't get to see anything," Johnny said as he kicked the dirt. I rubbed his head, messing up his hair.

Ron said, "Not only that, we met the Swamp People."

Maggie replied, "Yep, it's been a wild trip. I'm ready to go home."

I said, "Let's get the hell out of here." Adolf barked twice as if agreeing with me. Everyone laughed as we mounted up.

We finally reached I-75 and as we drove up the on ramp, in the dark, Tommy slammed on the brakes. The highway was blocked by cars, trucks, and people.

I told my crew to stay put while Mike, Tommy, and I walked up with Adolf to check out what was going on. As we walked up to the highway we observed a line of cars on south and north bound sides of the road. It looked like hundreds of people were camped along the side the Interstate.

Most of the people were sleeping but some were awake sitting around camp fires. No one paid any attention to us as we walked down the side of the highway. I had my M4 slung across my chest with my hand on the grip.

An old man walked up to me and Adolf didn't even growl. He asked, "Mister, you got any food or water you can spare?" He had no visible weapons and didn't seem a threat. He looked a little skinny and undernourished. I guessed he was about 75 years old.

The old man reached out and petted Adolf on the head. That was strange because Adolf doesn't let strangers touch him. I noticed Adolf even wagged his tail.

I replied, "No Sir, I don't."

He said, "It's not for me it's for my grandkids. Don't you have anything?"

"Tommy, you got any food on you?"

Tommy stepped up to him. "Here you go, Mister." He gave him a handful of energy bars.

"God Bless you both."

Mike gave him a bottle of water and asked him, "What's going on here? Why's everyone stopped?"

The old man replied, "Some men are blocking the road a few miles up ahead. They're taking everyone's guns and food. So our convoy stopped for the night. We're short on everything, food, water, and gas. Our people will clear the road block in the morning."

I asked, "Where are you from?" I already knew the answer by the license plate on his car.

"We're from New York State."

"Are you moving here because of the Arctic Vortex?"

"Yeah, that's right. It's damn cold up there right now. I've never seen snow in July before."

Mike asked, "Are all these cars in your convoy?"

"No. We have 45 vehicles in our group. I don't know who the other people are. They just stopped for the night like we did. We're all stuck here on the side of the road because of some damn bandits."

I pulled out a smoke and offered him one. He gladly took it and savored the taste as he took his first drag. Blowing out the smoke he asked,

"Where you boys from?"

Tommy said, "South of here."

"Oh, so you know your way around here."

"Yeah, a little bit."

I noticed there was a small crowd of people starting to gather around us. I didn't like getting circled by group of strange people. Tommy and Mike turned to face the small group with their M4's slung around chests. They were all asking the same questions. They wanted to know where they could obtain gas, food, and water.

Tommy whispered in my ear, "We have about 100 pounds of meat left and 15 gallons of water. We might as well give it to them."

I nodded my head. "Bring the truck up here and unload it."

Mike and I stood there answering all kinds of questions from the small group of people who seemed friendly enough. I didn't see anyone carrying a gun out in the open.

As our trucks pulled up everyone stepped aside. Tommy and Ron dropped the tail gate on the F-350. I told the crowd that we had some fairly fresh beef and to line up behind the truck to get a share.

The old man got pushed aside by the crowd. He didn't have the strength to push and shove his way into line. It made me a little angry that some of the people didn't show any respect for an old person.

I jumped in front of the line with my M4 and Adolf. That stopped everyone in their tracks. I told the old guy to come to the front on the line.

I handed him about five pounds of meat and said, "Come on, I'll help you carry this to your kids." Mike picked up a couple gallons of water and we followed him.

We walked him to his old car to make sure no one took his food. Mike asked, "What's your name?"

He replied, "Just call me Grandpa Jack."

I gave him a surprised look. "That's my name and I'm a Grandpa, also."

He nodded his head and said, "I know."

I attributed his comment to being an old man.

"Sir, I'm Mike." They shook hands and

exchanged nods.

"Well, it's sure a pleasure to meet you two Army men. I was in the Army once." We didn't have the heart to tell him we weren't really in the Army.

We reached his car, about 300 feet away, which was an old beat up Chevy. Two kids, a boy and a little girl, were waiting for him. They ran up and gave him a hug. "Kids, this is Jack and Mike. They're in the Army. God brought them here." I could tell they loved their Grandpa.

The kids both stuck out their hands. The boy said, "Hello Sir, my name is Adam." For some reason I shook his hand without fear of getting Ebola. Adam held out his hand for Adolf to smell. The big dog wagged his tail showing he liked Adam.

"My name is Emma. I'm eight years old," the little girl told us in a high pitched voice.

I picked her up and gave her a little hug. "It's nice to meet you Emma." She gave me a peck on the cheek. I put her down thinking what a cute kid. She had long curly brown hair and had on a sweatshirt that said New York.

Adam said, "I'm twelve." Adam was a big

kid for his age. He was almost as tall as me. He held himself straight and tall. He had blond hair and wore the same type of sweatshirt.

Grandpa directed Adam to start a fire. Mike and I helped him by finding some sticks and branches from nearby trees. Soon a fire was going. Grandpa cut up the meat like a real pro and soon beef steaks were on the fire cooking.

Old man Jack asked, "Aren't you boys gonna eat?"

"No thanks, we already ate," Mike said.

I warned Grandpa, "Be sure to cook that meat well, because it's been sitting a while."

He nodded his head while looking at me. "What do you mean a while?"

"We made the kill yesterday about 5 pm."

"It'll be fine."

While they were eating I asked, "Where are the kids' parents?"

"They passed on." That's all he said so I didn't push the issue with the kids around.

Looking at the eastern sky I could tell the sun would be coming up soon. Adam gave Adolf a small piece of meat which he swallowed without even chewing. The two children ate half a pound each. I could tell they were hungry. The kids finished eating and Grandpa told them to get some rest in the car. You could tell they were dead tired.

None of us spoke for a few minutes. We just sat there peering at the camp fire. Out of the silence Grandpa said, "I think God sent you."

I looked at him and asked, "Sir, why do you think that?"

"Because I've been praying for some time, ever since the kids' Dad and Mom were killed. I've been praying for God to save them."

"They have you to protect them," Mike said.

"No, not really. I don't have long. I should have been dead a month ago from the big 'C' but God has given me the strength to carry on for the kids."

"So tell me, why do you think God sent us?" I asked him again.

"Believe me. God sent you, Mr. Gunn. Is that spelled with one 'n' or two?"

"Two. How do you know my last name?"

"I had a dream. God told me that a solider would come to help us. His name would be the same as the weapon he carried in his hands. I knew it was you that God sent ... when I laid eyes on you. You might not know it but you're one of God's Warriors."

"I do believe in God and I do pray. But ... I'm nothing special. God has never talked to me."

Grandpa Jack asked me for another smoke. I handed it to him and lit him up. He commented, "God don't have to talk to you. He works his miracles through your actions."

I just sat there and couldn't respond. It was amazing that he knew my last name.

Finishing his smoke Grandpa Jack said, "I just want a normal safe life for my grandkids until they can fend for themselves."

"What do you mean a normal safe life? Nothing is normal anymore," I said.

"I'll explain more tomorrow. I gotta rest now." He went and laid down on the front seat of the car without saying another word.

Mike softly commented, "Man that was spooky. How the hell did he know your name?"

"I got no idea but maybe God did tell him. How else would he know?"

There was a little meat left so I gave another piece to Adolf. I thought it was strange that Adolf let the old man and Adam pet him without even a growl. He never does that. He never lets strangers touch him or me. I glanced at Adolf who wandered over to the open car door and laid down as if guarding our new friends.

Pointing to Adolf I said, "Mike, look at that."

"Yeah, he's taken a liking to them," he replied.

"Adolf never does that. He's always by my side. That's very weird. Something isn't right."

Tommy came over to the car and told us that all the meat had been handed out. The sun was just peeking over the horizon when Adolf let out a whimper. I looked over at him and he had his front paws on the seat near Grandpa Jack.

Then Adolf jumped inside the car. I went to check it out. As I approached, Adolf was whining, which I never heard him do before. He was looking at Grandpa. His big paws were on top of Jack's chest.

I leaned in the car looking at Grandpa. He didn't look good. I felt for a pulse. The old man was gone. He passed away in his sleep. He told us he didn't have long.

I whispered to Tommy, "Get a couple of shovels and a body bag so we can give him a decent burial."

Tommy quickly returned and we placed Grandpa in the bag. I began digging a hole, in the soft sandy soil, off the side of the road near some wild flowers. The kids woke up when they heard the noise. Adam asked, "What happened. Where's Grandpa at?"

I bent down on one knee and gathered both kids in my arms. I said, "Grandpa has gone to Heaven."

Emma said, "He's with Mommy and Daddy now."

Adam commented, "Grandpa won't be sick anymore."

I couldn't help but notice that neither of them cried. They didn't shed one tear. Maybe they had seen too much death in their short lives and had no more tears left.

"Here Adam, I found these on your

Grandpa." I gave Adam a gold cross which I found hanging on Jack's neck. It wasn't a normal cross. There was also a gold ring that was on his middle finger. They looked old and had some kind of writing on them, which I couldn't read.

"Thank you. My Grandfather wanted me to have these."

Tommy and Mike dug a deep grave and gently lowered the body in it. Then they proceeded to covered it up. By this time a number of people had gathered around to find out who died. As I advised each person it occurred to me I didn't even know his last name. I asked Adam, "What's your Grandpa's last name?"

"The same as mine … De Molay."

"What did your Grandpa do?"

"He was a Minister for Christ. It's a secret, but I guess I can tell you now. He was a Grand Master of the Knights Templar."

I looked at Adam and didn't say another word. Everyone knows the Knights Templar don't exist anymore. However, if my memory serves me right, Jacques de Molay was the last known Grand Master of the Knights. He was burned at the stake in France around thirteen hundred. I wondered if they were related.

A stranger came forward with a two foot high white cross to place at the grave. He had a can of paint and I asked him to write on the cross, 'Jack de Molay, Minister for God.'

I estimated that about a hundred people gathered around while I said a few simple words. "God, please take the soul of Jack de Molay into Heaven to be with his family. He was your loyal servant and follower. Amen." Adam and Emma placed wild flowers next to the cross and said their own silent prayers.

Others were standing there praying out loud or in silence. Soon all the people left, returning to their vehicles, except for one man and woman. Adam and Emma were hanging on to me when this couple walked up to us. The man said, "Don't worry, Mister. We'll take Adam and Emma with us. Come along now children."

They reached for the children. Adolf let out a deep growl and the strange people pulled back a step. I eyeballed the couple and guessed they were about 50 years old. They looked stern and fairly fit.

Emma and Adam didn't move and held on to me tighter. I could tell they didn't wanna go with these people. I said, "I don't think they wanna go with you."

"They have no choice. We're people of God and knew their Grandfather. We'll take good care of them."

"I believe you would take good care of them, but it was Jack's wish that the children stay with me. God told him that I would be their protector."

"You! Look at you. You're just a hired gun. A killer no doubt. God wouldn't want that. You're not even part of our group."

Adam spoke up. "It's true. Grandpa told me that this is the man God sent to watch over us. We have to stay with him. It's God's wish." With that comment the couple stormed away in a fit of anger.

What Adam said really set in and bothered me. It's God's wish that I watch over them. Why did God select me, of all people? The couple was right, I have killed many people over the years, but only those who deserved it. What's so special about these two kids?

I came to my senses. I had to stop thinking

about how weird this whole thing was or it would drive me nuts. I said, "Ok, kids get your stuff out of the car and let's go. Don't worry, everything is going to be fine."

Adam asked, "What about the car?"

"We'll leave it; maybe someone else can use it."

The kids picked up their gear which consisted of four bags. Adam also carried a long case. I asked him, "What's in the case?"

"It's my Grandpa's sword."

I didn't say another word as we walked to the trucks but it made me wonder what the sword was for. Arriving at our vehicles, I introduce them to Johnny and the rest of the crew. Maggie and Lisa were really happy to help them out because they loved kids, even if they had none of their own.

Tommy stood up on the roof of the Hummer looking around. "Man, cars are backed up as far as I can see. We're gonna have to drive in the median to get past this traffic jam." He slipped back into the gun turret. We were ready to move out.

Out of nowhere, a large group of people came running up and stood in front of our trucks. They blocked our exit. At the head of the group were the man and woman who wanted to take the kids.

The man yelled, "You're not going anywhere until you hand over those children." I estimated there were possibly thirty people standing in our way. I scanned the group for weapons, but didn't see any.

I climbed out of the truck and approached him. "Sir, we already had this discussion. Grandpa Jack wanted the kids to go with me. Adam even told you that."

Then to my surprise Adam got out and climbed up on the hood so the crowd could see him. Adam shouted, "He's right! It was my Grandfathers wish and a command from God!"

"The man yelled, "How do we know that?"

"Please listen to me. It's God's wish that we go with Mr. Gunn and start a new Templar Order. You need to select a new Grand Master. That's all I have to say, so please let us pass in peace."

A new Templar Order? What the hell is the kid talking about?

Someone yelled, "Go in peace, Adam. May God continue to bless you."

The entire crowd yelled, "God Bless you!"

Another man said, "Sorry but you can't leave yet. The men are still blocking the road and it's too dangerous. Let the Knights clear the road before you leave. We'll make the army ready and remove the heathens."

The crowd quickly dispersed. I was amazed at how well Adam spoke to the group. He was a natural leader and speaker. When he spoke people listened to him. He clearly had some power and respect of the people despite his young age.

Adam said, "We should stay here until the Templar Army opens up the road block."

What army? What's this kid talking about?

"Ok, but where's the army?" I asked.

Adam smiled and replied, "Just watch."

We all dismounted. Maggie had her arm around Adam and Lisa had Emma on her knee. Johnny, while holding my hand, asked, "What's going on, Grandpa?"

"We're waiting for the Templar Knights to clear the road block."

"What are the Templar Knights?"

"It's hard to explain, but look … there they are." I lifted Johnny up on the hood of the Hummer so he could see them.

What a spectacular sight it was. Row upon row of men dressed in snow white mantles with a Crimson Cross on the front marching to a drum beat. Some men were flying flags but all of them carried rifles. Many had big swords hanging from their belts. As they marched down the center of the highway, I jumped on the hood to see them better.

"So the Knights are some kind of soldiers?" Johnny asked.

"Yeah, that's right," I said.

I estimated there were about 100 men. I asked Adam, "Do they really know how to fight?"

Adam replied, "The Templar Knights have been fighting a thousand years for God. They protect people from evil forces. This Order has seen a lot of combat over the last few years since the collapse of the government."

"I'll be damned," Tommy said. Everyone else in my crew was speechless.

"Yeah, it's amazing the Knights Templar still exist," I stated.

I had read a lot of stories about the Knights Templar. They were brave men fighting against evil. The Templar headquarters was located on the Temple Mount in Jerusalem. They were the ultimate warriors who were not afraid to die for their faith.

An hour later we began to hear sporadic gunfire. It became more intense for about 15 minutes and then suddenly ceased. Sometime later a man wearing the white mantle with the Crimson Cross came running over to us.

Out of breath, he reported to Adam. "The road block has been removed. You can proceed. Go in peace Adam de Molay." The solider left and milled around telling everyone to get ready to move out.

I said, "Ok, let's mount up and go home." I was relieved that we didn't have to fight our way through the road block with kids along. Their safety was my primary concern.

We drove down the median passing the long convoy. Reaching the road block we observed that a few Knights had been killed. The men who put up the road block were the same ones we had a run in with yesterday. We stopped to survey the situation.

I pointed and said, "Look, there's Sam Smith." The Knights had all the prisoners lined up.

They where cutting off their heads, one by one, using the big swords. We pulled away rather quickly so the children wouldn't see the bloodshed. It was clear to me that the Templar Army was no one to fuck with. They didn't take any prisoners or show mercy to those who opposed them. I was impressed to say the least.

The kids were piled in the back of my Hummer along with Adolf. Adam asked, "Where are we going?"

I replied, "We're going home to Tocabaga."

"How far is it?"

"Not far from here. We'll be there in a couple of hours."

A half hour later Adam shouted. "Look! Over there, in the field. There's two deer." Our little convoy pulled over to the side of the road.

"You got good eyes, Adam," I said.

"I can take them out from here," Tommy said, as he set up his rifle.

We managed to bag the two deer, load them up, and get on the way in less than an hour. At least we weren't going back to Tocabaga empty-handed. Maybe we'd have enough meat to feed our people one meal.

Driving back home there was more traffic than normal. The traffic reminded me of the good old days when hundreds of cars zoomed down I-75. We must have passed a hundred cars with no incidents. People stranded on the roadside waved at us as we passed trying to get us to stop. Their plates told us they were all from up north. More than likely they had run out of gas. We couldn't stop to help anyone.

It was clear to me that the Arctic Vortex was affecting a lot of people. The Hordes were coming which would affect everything. It would cause fuel shortages. Food and water would become scarce. It would drive more people south creating a higher level of danger. People do crazy things when they are starving to death. It occurred to me that the Vortex might come this far south so we'd have to take precautions in case it gets really cold.

We arrived back on Tocabaga safely. It felt great to be home. I could let my guard down and relax. I had a lot to think about. I wondered if our new family members would fit in. I figured Emma would be ok, but I didn't know about Adam. He was wise beyond his years.

He didn't act like or even talk like a kid. I needed a little one on one time with Adam. I needed to figure him out. What makes him tick? What is that little brain of mush thinking? Does he want to start a Templar Order on Tocabaga?

Carlos took the deer to Steve to be butchered. Everyone else went to the Green Room for a drink but Ron, Tommy, and I went home. We were dead tired as we walked in the door with the kids. I yelled, "Surprise Honey, we're home! We have some new family members."

The women took Adam and Emma, introduced them to the other kids, and got them set up in a bedroom. We were running out of room. Now we had eight kids to raise and protect. A big responsibility for sure, but with the help of all the family adults we would manage.

It was getting late so the men in my family went to the Green Room for a night-cap. I just had one drink and went home to bed. It was almost 10 pm when I walked in the door.

Hemmi said, "I need to talk to you. Let's go outside."

It was a cool night, cooler than normal. I noticed the humidity was lower making it almost necessary to wear a jacket. Was the Vortex coming?

An owl hooted and I could hear his wings

flapping in the night stillness as he flew close by. Adolf sat up when we came out on the patio. He looked at us and then laid back down, when he felt everything was ok. Adolf guards our back door which we leave unlocked. No one would dare try to enter his territory.

Sitting down, in my squeaky 20 year-old rocking chair, I lit up one more smoke and asked. "Ok, Honey, what's up?"

Hemmi pulled up a chair close to me and whispered. "Jack, there's something wrong with Adam. I went to help him take off his shirt and saw that he has scars all over his back. He's been whipped with something."

"Whipped?"

"Yeah, he has big ugly long scars all over his back."

I didn't know what to make of this. I said, "Ok, tomorrow I'll ask him how he got the scars."

"Just do it in a nice way. I think he has some mental issues."

"Why do you say that?"

"There's just something about him. The way he acts and speaks. I hate to say it, but he's kinda

136

creepy."

I nodded my head. "Well, let me tell you how we found him …" I proceeded to tell her the whole story about Jack de Molay and the Knights Templar.

Hemmi sat there with her mouth open listening to me. When I finished she said, "Holy shit. Do you believe that God spoke to the old man?"

"Yeah. How else would he know my name?"

Hemmi replied, "I think his Grandfather and maybe his Father were religious nuts. I think they tried to beat their ideas and teachings into him. Now he's a nut case also."

Hemmi was probably right about his Grandpa but he seemed like such a nice old man. Of course, I only knew him a few hours. I do know that Adam is a little weird.

I said, "Let's talk some more tomorrow. I need some rest."

Hemmi grabbed my hand. "Let's get some sleep."

As I walked past the bedroom that Johnny,

Jimmy, and Adam were sharing I cracked the door a little and peeked in. Adam was on the floor next to his bed. His hands were folded and he was praying. I wondered how long he had been kneeling there.

Adam turned his head and gazed at me for a second. He didn't say a word to me and kept on praying. His gaze was strange to say the least. He looked like he was in a trance.

I went to bed but couldn't fall sleep. The kid had me freaked out. I got up and went to the kitchen for a double shot of JD. Maybe it would help me sleep.

AUGUST 4, 2025

I woke up feeling like crap. I was in a bad mood because of the lack of sleep. I needed food and a cup of mud to boost my energy level. It was 8 am and all the children were up and running around.

Johnny, along with the rest of the kids, came running into the kitchen. He asked, "Grandpa, is it ok if we show Adam and Emma around Tocabaga?"

"Go ahead, but don't go to the Fort, and stay away from the water. Oh, and watch out for snakes."

"Ok, Grandpa." They took off running out the door.

"Maybe if Adam hangs around normal kids he'll start acting more like a kid. I'll talk to him later. Let's see how he does today," I told my wife.

After some chow I took Adolf and went on a patrol around the island. I wanted to follow the kids, at a distance, to see where they were going. I really wanted to keep an eye Adam. He was older, bigger, smarter, and stronger than the other children.

At the island central kitchen, Steve was butchering one of the deer. I asked him how many dinners could he make from the meat. He told me there was about 200 pounds of good meat, which would make one small meal for everyone. He would also stretch it by making soup out of the scraps and bones.

At least we have plenty of other protein from fish and chickens. Our farm is a gift from God. It gives us a bounty of good vegetables and fruit every day. We could have it a lot worst like the poor fools moving here from up north.

It occurred to me that if the Vortex comes here we could lose all our vegetables and fruit. I made a mental note to ask the women to start canning as much as they could. We would also need to stock up on firewood which would mean dangerous trips to cut down trees.

I had no idea how cold it could become, but I did know from past experience that it can get to freezing here. About 30 years ago it actually snowed in St. Petersburg. The snow only lasted a day but it was freezing cold for two weeks.

Normally, a cold front takes five days to a

week to reach our area from the Great Lakes region. Most of the time fronts stop a 100 miles north of here. It still gets cold on Tocabaga, maybe down to 40 degrees, but it never reaches freezing. The warm water surrounding the island helps fend off a deep freeze. Forty degrees is still cold and can make you very uncomfortable.

Following the kids at a discrete distance, while making my security checks, I saw them all run home. It was lunch time and growing kids never miss a meal. I finished my rounds and went home for lunch.

By the time I arrived home the kids had already ate lunch. It was Saturday so there wasn't any school and they were hanging around the house. Adam was sitting on the patio looking at some of our family pictures hanging on the wall. I joined him figuring it was a good time to do some bonding.

I had just sat down next to Adam when Johnny and Jimmy came in. "Adam, come on we're gonna play some ball."

Adam looked at me and then at Johnny. "No thanks." The boys ran off with their ball, gloves, and bat.

I asked Adam, "Why don't you go play ball with the boys?"

"I would, but I don't know how."

"You don't know how to play baseball?"

Adam fidgeted around with his fingers. "No, I don't know how. Grandpa never taught me. Grandpa thought it was a waste of time."

I put my hand on his shoulder. "That's ok, a lot of people don't play ball. What did Grandpa teach you?"

Adam looked around the room as if trying to think of a reply. "He taught me many things. I know a lot about U.S. history, math, reading, and the Templars of course. I learned fencing, shooting, and hand-to-hand combat."

"What type of hand-to-hand combat do you know?"

"I know an ancient fighting method first used by the Knights Templar."

"That sounds awesome. Maybe you can show me some moves sometime."

Adam enthusiastically replied, "I'd be happy to do that."

Adam reached down and petted Adolf. "I really like this dog."

"He likes you too." We sat there for a few minutes while I comtemplated how to word my next question. "Adam, can you tell me what happen to your Father and Mother?"

"They were killed by some guy who broke into our house."

"I'm sorry to hear that."

"Lucky for me and Emma, we weren't there when it happened. We were staying with Grandpa at the time."

"So how long did you live with Grandpa?"

"Since I was eight."

"Adam, please tell me how you got those scars on your back."

"My Dad whipped me. He used to say he was beating the devil out of me. He said it made me a better person and follower of God."

"Did Grandpa ever beat you or Emma?"

"Well, sometimes … but only if we were bad."

I couldn't think of anything to say. I pondered the idea that Adam's Father was a real nut case. Maybe his Grandpa killed his own son to protect Adam. I'll never know what really happened. Still a person who has been abused tends to abuse others. I need to keep any eye on Adam.

Adam asked, "Do you have school here?"

"Monday through Friday all the kids go to school. I think you'll like it. Older kids your age get to pick a job skill to learn. We have fishing, farming, hunting, cooking, and security jobs you can learn. Here on Tocabaga, everyone is expected to contribute for our survival."

"That sounds great. I'm interested in following God's path. Do you have a minister?"

"No, but we have a church. Come on, I'll show it to you."

Adam, along with Adolf, followed me outside. We walked to the church which took about 15 minutes.

As we toured the church, Adam said, "Maybe I can be your minister."

"Yeah, that might be possible when you're older."

Adam nodded his head. "Who's in charge of security?"

I seemed to be making progress bonding with him. "I'm Director of Security. I was elected to a four-year term. We have elections here and try to follow normal laws and the Constitution."

"Maybe I can be the Security Director. When I'm older, of course."

I kinda looked at him and said, "No one wants to be Director of Security."

The kid had big ambitions. He wanted to be a minister and Head of Security. He was already thinking way ahead. He was thinking out of the box. It made me curious what he was really thinking. I didn't like the fact that he was looking so far into the future. Normal kids his age never worry about such things.

"Why doesn't anyone want to be the Head of Security?" he asked.

"It's a tough job and demands a lot of your time."

Adam nodded. "Yeah, it's not a job for everyone."

We silently sat in the church for a few

minutes and I decided to press the issue about the Templar Knights. "Adam, tell me about the Knights Templar."

Adam looked at me and didn't answer right away. I guess he was thinking what to tell me. "The Templar Order is a secret society. We are on a mission for God. The Knights Templar main mission is to restore the United States of America to be One Nation Under God. We will help restore our country to its greatness. We are a country founded on Christian-Judeo beliefs."

"I like that … but how will you do that?" Now I was really concerned about what he was planning. He's just a kid and thinking this way could be dangerous.

Adam gave a sigh, like it was all too boring for him to explain to me. "Ok, I'll tell you the theory or premise since you're my guardian. The reason the country fell apart is because we lost our way. We lost our direction and didn't follow God's teachings or commandments. The country became evil.

"We removed prayers from schools and removed the word God or Christ from our books. We didn't teach anything about Christ or God. We took down the Ten Commandments from courtrooms and schools. We took the Christ out of

Christmas and made it just another holiday."

"Yes, that's all true," I replied. "Tell me more."

"The Templar Knights are God's warriors. We must destroy any person who does not believe in God. There must be a purging of the evil ones from the United States."

Holy Shit! This kid is nuts. I needed to hear more. "How are you going to purge the evil ones?"

Adam was now walking around in circles as if worked up into a frenzy. "The Templar Army is now spreading out across the United States. The Order I was with will be based in Florida, just south of here, in Bradenton where Hernando de Soto landed in America in 1539. De Soto was a Templar Knight. In due time, I will start another Order enlisting at least a thousand men."

This kid has been brain-washed by his Father and Grandpa into thinking he would be the savior of the United States. I felt sorry for him because I knew his brain was consumed with the idea he was God's Warrior. I now felt Adam could be very dangerous to have on Tocabaga.

Adam continued by asking, "Do you believe in reincarnation?"

"By reincarnation do you mean coming back to life in a different body?"

"Yes, that's what I mean."

"Well, I don't know since I've never died, as far as I know." I gave a little chuckle thinking what I said was funny.

Adam looked at me with a stern face. "Jesus was born again. He came back reincarnated after three days in a different body so no one but his close friends would know who he was. Then he ascended to heaven changing back to the God. I'm living proof of reincarnation. I was reincarnated from the Jacques de Molay blood line as was my Father and Grandfather."

"Adam, exactly how do you know that?"

"I know that because secrets and ancient relics have been passed down over the generations. We have the Templar's Treasure Hoard."

"If you have the Templar's Treasure taken from Jerusalem, tell me about it."

"I can't tell you, it's a secret. Only a few people know what it is. I can tell you the items in the Hoard prove that God is real. It verifies the Old and New Testament."

"Ok, I believe in God. You don't need to convince me. What I don't agree with is what you wanna do. You want to destroy anyone who does not believe in God. That's not what the United States is about. We have freedom of religious expression to believe in God or not. The country was founded by pilgrims fleeing religious persecution."

I hoped what I said would sink into his brain. His thinking was way out there.

Adam responded, "Yes, I know all that, but we need to go to extremes to bring us back to normal. What about people like radical Islamists? There's al Qaida and ISIS who would gladly cut off your head if you don't convert to their form of Islam."

"We've done battle with al Qaida. I agree they need to be eliminated. Perhaps you need to lead your Templars in that direction. To me, that makes a lot more sense."

Adam stopped pacing and sat down. He seemed to be contemplating what I had just told him. "What you say is true. They will be our first target," Adam said.

I replied, "They should be your only target. You can't go around killing people because they don't believe in God. You'll make a lot of enemies including the United States Army and the people living here on Tocabaga."

Adam replied, "You've given me a lot to think about. I'll pray and see what God tells me."

"Ok, you pray on it. It's getting late, so let's go home."

On the way home Adam said, "Thank you for the talk. You remind me of my Grandpa."

I didn't say a word as I put my arm around his shoulder and we slowly walked home.

I never thought this kid would be a big nut case, but he was messed up. On the other hand it would be nice to have a counter force to fight the never ending attacks of the radical forces of ISIS and al Qaida. There are thousands of them slowly taking over parts of the country to create their own Islamic State. The Knights Templar could help quell the extremists. However, based on what Adam told me he's also an extremist.

We arrived home and ate dinner. I usually say the prayer at dinner but I let Adam say grace. After eating, I rounded up my male family members and we went to the Green Room. I had to tell them what Adam had revealed to me. I needed to seek some advice on what to do with Adam.

I informed them what Adam was thinking and everyone was pretty much surprised. Ron commented that the kid freaked him out. Tommy told us Adam would probably outgrow the ideas that were drummed into his head by his Grandfather.

I told them that I didn't think he'd outgrow his crazy ideas. They were beaten into him. He's been mentally damaged. I suggested we need to keep Adam busy all the time so he can't dwell on being a Templar Knight. We needed to have him go fishing, farming, hunting, and even start him on guard duty training. These activities along with his schooling might help him. I asked my family to tell their wives about Adam and to keep a close eye on him.

I sat alone on the patio having a smoke while writing a work schedule for Adam. I'll keep him very busy like the other kids. The only difference is he'll be closely monitored.

God hasn't spoken to me yet, so in the mean-time I'll do what I think is best for Adam and Tocabaga. Maybe I'll pray a little more.

If you have any ideas on what I should do to help Adam please email me.

Email me at <u>tocabaga.jack@gmail.com</u>.   I WILL REPLY.

That's all for now.

GOD BLESS AMERICA, LAND OF THE FREE, and HOME OF THE BRAVE!

Jack Gunn

DRAMATIS PERSONAE

TOCABAGA

Adam de Molay – A future Knights Templar leader. Sent to Jack by God.

Albert Madison – Navy Vet. who comes to Tocabaga with his wife and two kids

Army Mike – Retired Army combat vet, we just call him Mike

Barry – A quisling killed by the Gunn family

Billy – Kid found living on the street with his sister Rosie and brother Peter

Brogan – A Tocabaga security guard who went MIA

Bok Lam – A Chinese man and close friend of Jack's since high school

Buck – Motorcycle gang leader killed by Maggie

Chase – A quisling

Colonel Turner – Commanding Officer of the Army Rangers based at Fort Desoto

Colonel Park - aka Captain Kim a South Korean

spy working for China

Corporal Phillips – In charge of the communications office at Fort Desoto

Captain Sessions – Combat officer, commands and controls combat operations in the field

Captain Riley – Female tank commander, girl friend of Captain Sessions

Captain Zhu Lei – A commie killed by Tommy

Chris – Tocabaga security guard and close friend of Jack

Daniel Gibbs – Bad guy from a convoy on Interstate 75

Dew – A quisling killed by the Gunn family

Dr. Carl Urban – The inventor of the RCCD Units and friend of Jack's

Dr. Carl Urban, Jr. – Son of Dr. Urban

Dr. Alvin Sinclair – Robot inventor and Commie killed by Jack

Ellen – A lonely woman

Emma de Molay – The sister of Adam found on Interstate 75

First Lt. Fisher – TALOS Warrior, Platoon commander

Farmer John – An old farmer saved by Jack, now living on Tocabaga

Guy Allen or **GA** – Suspected spy living on Tocabaga was killed by Jack

General Chen – A Red Chinese Army General in charge of the Florida invasion force

General Harper – Commander of the Rangers located at SOCOM

George Taylor – A nice kid who was bullied in school by Nick

Grandpa Jack – Jack de Moley the Knights Templar Grand Master

Hemmi – Wife of Jack Gunn

Joe – RCCD tech. Supervisor; a tough guy killed by Jack

Little Johnny – Adopted grandson of Jack's

Johnny the Fisherman – A quisling killed by security

Jill – A warrior killed by Feds

Jim Bo – Husband to Amy and son-in-law of Jack

Jimmy Smith – A bully from years ago

Ken – US Deputy Marshal who went missing

Leroy – The man who killed Jack's little brother Mike

Lee – A Chinese invisible

Mike – Jack Gunn's little brother killed by a doper

Maggie – Wife of Robbie, who is in charge of the farming

Mr. Johnson or **Famer John** – Old time Farmer

Mr. Horn – Pig farmer and dirt bag who wanted to kidnap Maggie for breeding

Nick – A bully from Junior High School

Peter – Little nine year old brother to Rosie

Rosie – A fifteen year old girl Jack found living on the street

Robbie – Best friend of Jack Gunn, a Tocabaga security guard killed by the FPF on April 27, 2025

Ron – Brother of Jack Gunn Retired Navy vet. Part of Tocabaga security.

Rick – President of Tocabaga Association, security team member

Sam Smith – Leader of a convoy of bad dangerous people

Sally – A warrior killed by Feds

Scotty – A quisling killed by security

Sergeant Hammer – Army Ranger

Sergeant First Class Dale – killed in action

Sergeant Major Willis – Ranger squad leader and security guard for Jack

Sergeant Cain – the Drone Master

Sergeant Smith - Army Ranger assigned as security guard for Jack

Stan – Deputy Marshal

Sue – Wife of Albert Madison

Tommy Gunn – Son of Jack Gunn and a retired Marine Scout Sniper

Tony – Bar keeper and sharp-shooter for Tocabaga security

Trini – Amazon Warrior who killed Troy

Troy – A quisling killed by security

Victor Elway – An old farmer from Ellenton now living on Tocabaga with his friend Farmer John

Zack – A quisling killed by the Gunn family

TOCABAGA 9: THE CRIMSON CROSS

www.ingramcontent.com/pod-product-compliance
Lightning Source LLC
Chambersburg PA
CBHW051522170626
46811CB00002B/949